Sheriff Tom
Vs.
The Zombies

By
Nick Kisella

Based on the screenplay by
Ryan Scott Weber

First printing

A Weber Pictures Novel
Nick Kisella's photo by Stan Stronski
Ryan Scott Weber's photo by Michael Enoches

Dedications

Nick Kisella:

To Kimberly and the twins
My inspiration and strength
To Ryan and everyone involved with the film
Yet another, Rich
Miss you

Ryan Scott Weber:

To my Grandparents Ron and Filomena for all your support and inspiration.
Kristen for all her hard work and love, Sean and Angie Campbell, the cast and crew of this film, Rocko the dog,
The Brady's. Joe Parascand for his dedication and hard work bringing Sheriff Tom to life.

Prelude

The Day After Mary Horror

The streets of Bernardsville seemed oddly empty as Joao Carlos Silva navigated his Purple Hundai Accent through town. It was the day after 'Mary Horror Night', and there was more than the typical trash; some of the vending tables were still set up, which according to a town ordinance wasn't supposed to happen. Usually the streets were still crowded with tourists and a stray reporter here and there trying to uncover new information about the infamous murderess or her family, but all he saw was emptiness.

Joao Carlos, or JC, as he was more widely known, knew better than to work the night of the actual event, which he had made the mistake of doing the previous year. Being the owner of the most popular pub in town, it was a night that didn't end well at all, with him having to throw out nearly a dozen drunken patrons after a fight broke out.

"Damn kids, arguing about whether 'Mary Horror' liked men or women." JC muttered to himself, backing his car up to the rear of the pub. "As if it would even matter, idiots." He declared with an annoyed sigh.

JC dismissed his questions about the unlikely state of the streets to focus on the job at hand, and began his normal routine. He unlocked the back door of the pub, punched in a quick alarm code and then unloaded the fresh vegetables he'd picked up from the local farmer's market on the way in. He left them in the walk-in fridge for the cook to use in his salads, and finally entered the bar area, where he felt most at home.

He liked the bar, the people, atmosphere. Being a bartender kept him on his toes and always in a rush. He enjoyed that along with hearing all the town gossip. JC knew more about the town and its elected officials than anyone, being asked more than once for advice on things he by no means should have been giving advice, much less known about. He even remembered when two EMTs, Jimmy and Billy came in the night all the 'Mary Horror' insanity started. They were regulars, but they got so trashed that night he had to drive them home himself, hearing about all the blood and gore at the Horowitz house.

After flipping over a few barstools, he flicked on the master-switch for the televisions situated over and around the bar, eyes immediately drawn to the screen facing him and the live news report flashing on the screen.

"What the hell-" JC muttered under his breath, absently walking closer to the television.

"This is Chuck Marble with a Special Report from News 25. Mary Horowitz was a high school senior accused of killing her entire family in her Bernardsville, New Jersey home." As the news anchorman narrated, a montage of photos flashed across the screen, showing Mary and her family, and then a picture of Sheriff Tom Walker is superimposed in the corner of the screen. A recording of his initial call from the crime scene began to play in the background.

"We've got a multiple homicide at the Horowitz place. There's blood and body parts everywhere." The Sheriff said, sounding out of breath.

When the recording cut out, more photos flashed across the screen, some of Mary and her mother, and several pictures of an old looking book with a strange symbol on the cover, and then the anchorman continued on.

"Mary Horowitz, dubbed 'Mary Horror' was reportedly possessed by a spell book passed down to her from her family, descendants of witches that somehow enabled her to come back to life after an apparent suicide as some sort of zombie, and go on a rampage, killing twelve people in all. We now take you live to news correspondent Lonnie Anderson, who is at the Horowitz house with two eyewitnesses."

The screen flashes to the front of the Horowitz house, where Lonnie Anderson is interviewing his two witnesses.

"I'm here with Billy Lloyd and Jimmy Jones, at the Horowitz house. Guys, can you tell me exactly what you saw shortly before dawn this morning?"

"Jesus Christ, that's Billy and Jimmy, and they're drunk!" Entranced, JC pulled up a barstool and sat down, eyes never leaving the screen.

Billy, clearly inebriated and still holding an empty beer bottle, staggered forward, then leaned heavily into Jimmy, who also wasn't very steady on his feet.

"You're Loni Anderson?" He pointed a shaky finger at the reporter and scrunched up his face. "I thought you were a much older woman-"

Jimmy cut him off with a slap to his arm.

"Shhhh," he said, holding a finger over his lips. "She's dead."

"She's not dead." Billy replied, annoyed.

"Guys, please, get it together here." Anderson spoke up loudly. "Can you tell me exactly what went down here? What did you see?"

"We, we saw lots of things." Billy's words were slurred, but his eyes were steady and focused on Lonnie. "We saw Mary, we saw Mary Horror." He pronounced 'horror' with a few too many 'r's, then flung his arm around Jimmy to steady himself again and continued on. "We saw Mary go into the house and shut the door,"

he pointed to the woods across the street. "Then Sheriff Tom came out, and he's screaming like a girl, 'Mary, Mary', and then," he started pointing at Jimmy, looking as if he were stabbing at him. "Tell him what happened dude, tell him what happened."

"What happened?" Anderson asked.

Jimmy looked at Anderson and grinned.

"He's dead." He replied.

"He died." Billy confirmed with a straight face.

"The Sheriff?" Anderson asked?

"Yeah," Jimmy said.

"No, we don't know," Billy said, "We saw him though, and then what happened. Tell him what happened after that." He started laughing.

"Well, after that I shit my pants." Jimmy stared directly into the camera when he said it, and there was no time for it to get it beeped out, so Anderson just tried to play it off as a joke and tried not to look too worried about losing his job.

"Well that's a little too much information right there." He turned toward the camera man, look slightly nervous. "And there you have it. Let's get back to Chuck at the studio."

As the camera faded into another montage of scenes it was clear that Billy had collapsed behind Anderson, pulling Jimmy down with him. Chuck Marble's narration continued as new images flickered on the screen.

"Experts in the paranormal field believe Mary has now just become a spirit that haunts the family home. Sheriff Tom Walker reportedly tried to stop her, and was last seen near the house, but there has been no sign of him, nor his body since. Efforts are still being made to locate him."

"Shit! What the hell have you guys gotten yourselves into this time?" JC said, shaking his head.

*****

Sheriff Tom howled angrily into the night, staring at the fiery moon high in the sky, the fresh wound in his back still throbbing with agony. He was about to throw a fist in the air and curse at God himself for allowing a foul creature like Mary Horror to exist when suddenly energy crackled. His hand glowed with it as if he'd been struck by lightning. For a split second he thought he felt hands on his back, near his wound, but ignored the sensation, reveling in the energy coursing through him.

Walker grunted with the jolt of pain it caused him, but it wasn't the same kind of pain he'd felt when Mary injured him with her notorious cleaver, or even when she'd torn out his left eye with her teeth early that evening. The sight of his own eye on the ground directly in front of his face still sent a chill up his spine.

As the energy surged through him he felt empowered, and the pain from his wounds vanished. So had Mary. With his renewed strength, he knew what he had to do, or as he'd suddenly thought, 'I've got to finish this.'

"Mary!" He called out angrily, turning to run toward the Horowitz house. He raced through the woods, legs pumping like pistons, with strength he didn't know he had left. He weaved through a close group of trees and could see the street in the distance over the hill of the Horowitz's front lawn as the sun started to come up, but stopped dead in his tracks.

An unearthly fog rapidly rolled in, billowing around him and glowing eerily as the final moments of the night passed. The silhouette of a young girl stood out in the pale luminance.

"Get the book Daddy, it's yours." The girl said, stepping out of the fog, where he could see her more clearly.

"Becky!" Sheriff Tom recognized the sound of her voice, and seeing her, his daughter, still so precious in his heart, made him angrier still at the abomination he was set to destroy. "Mary!" He growled with determination, running through the fog and the apparition of his daughter.

Sheriff Tom, so focused on his objective, crossed the lawn and reached the front steps of the house without even realizing it. He didn't see the car parked a short distance down the street with Billy Lloyd and Jimmy Jones sitting on the hood drinking beer. He just flung open the front door, swinging the shotgun he still carried around, shouting 'Mary'.

The first corpse he saw was Kim Fines. He saw her body, not her head, and didn't even care where it was.

"Damn 'Sparkle Bitch'," he muttered, stepping over her to search the rest of the ground floor. All the while, he kept hearing his daughter's voice ringing in his ears, 'Get the book Daddy, it's yours'. It felt like a mantra to him as he raced around the house, finally completing the circle and taking to the stairs. He stopped short when he saw the body of Jeff Horowitz, Mary's father, at the top of the stairs covered in blood. Out of the corner of his good eye he saw a flurry of movement in the foyer, and twisted around to see what it was.

There was nothing there, but his eye widened when he spotted exactly what he wanted sitting on top of a small table next to a lamp.

The spell book!

Sheriff Tom ran to it and snatched it off the top of the table, continuing on to the door and racing outside. He ran down and across the street, finally spotting Billy and Jimmy, totally drunk by then. He paused for a second, standing in front of their car, holding the shotgun and the book.

Jimmy's eyes bugged out in terror at the sight of Sheriff Tom, and what he thought was a bad case of gas turned out to be so much more.

"You fuckers!" The sheriff growled, turning to run off again just as Jimmy slipped and fell off the hood of the car.

Billy sat up with a loud belch. He looked around, sunglasses crooked on his face.

"Who, what the fuck was that?" He said, words slurred. He looked around in a panic. "Something really smells bad, smells like shit! Hey, Jimmy where the fuck are you?"

Billy felt himself slowly slide off the car and couldn't do anything to stop himself. He fell flat on his ass as Sheriff Tom ran through the woods.

ONE

The car that sped its way toward Bernardsville was old, primer gray, but fast. A sleeper in the truest sense of the word, it could roar like a lion. You wouldn't want to race it at a red light because even unpainted and seemingly outdated, it could blow even some of the most jacked new foreign cars out of the water.

Johnny, the driver, absently rubbed the stubble on his head, always proud of the 'buzz-cut' and how easy it was to maintain in his line of work. He was nearing thirty, loved rebuilding old cars, especially as a profession, and thought tattoos were a sincere form of art. That was evident by the dozen or so he had just on his arms alone. He'd heard about 'Mary Horror Night' a few weeks earlier and even picked up a flyer for it at one of the auto parts stores he frequented. He was looking forward to going, seeing how crazy people could act in public was a favorite pastime, especially when alcohol and maybe even a little pot were involved. And most especially with the bombshell of a sweetheart he had in his car as a passenger. 'There's nobody sweeter than Rose', he thought to himself.

"I really want to go to this party tonight." Rose, Johnny's 'bombshell' said above the cranked up music. She was in her mid-twenties, and looked as if she had stepped right out of a pin-up magazine from World War II. Her hair was long, and so light it was nearly white, with waves and curls perfectly in line with the contours of her face, which had been done up meticulously with just a tiny bit a make-up around her eyes because her skin was just that perfect. A thin swipe of lipstick gave her the ideal finishing touch and any 'Barbie' would be envious to see her. She had no ego about it, but rather considered herself lucky and enjoyed being herself, comfortable in her own skin.

She picked up the flyer from the dashboard and looked it over again for the umpteenth time, dropping it on the seat between them.

"Raise Mary Horror from the dead," she whispered, reciting the top line of the flyer.

Johnny looked over and nodded to her.

"C'mon, you really think they're going to raise Mary from the dead?" His grin was crooked, but he couldn't help but smile afterward just because he liked how Rose looked in his car.

"You never know." Rose shrugged her shoulders slightly, winking at him. "I heard she already came back from the dead once. It was last year, when all those people got killed, even the Mayor. They never solved those murders, it was on the news."

"Hey, at least there's free beer if it doesn't work." Johnny nodded. A flash of light suddenly caught his eye in the rearview mirror. He squinted at the mirror for a second then shook his head, frustrated.

"Damn it, I think I'm fuckin' getting' pulled over." He smacked the steering wheel. "Yep!" he confirmed, clenching an angry fist. "This is bullshit!"

Johnny eased the car over to the side of the road as the spinning red light shined behind him. He could hear the siren increase in volume as the car pulled up closer. 'Well, it *was* a perfect night', Johnny thought to himself as he heard the officer get out of his car.

"Shit." Johnny said flatly, rubbing his goatee to prevent himself from punching the steering wheel repeatedly.

"Just be cool Johnny," Rose said nervously, watching the shadow of the officer as he approached their car.

"I fuckin' hate cops." Johnny said, leaning back in the seat, staring at the ceiling. He could hear the gravel under the officers' shoes and it felt like nails on a chalkboard to him.

The beam of a flashlight hit Johnny full in the face, obscuring his view of the officer and momentarily blinding him.

"License and registration." The officer said mechanically with a deep gravelly voice.

Johnny pulled back, away from the light, blinking painfully and trying not to curse.

"What did I do wrong?" He asked calmly.

Sheriff Tom Walker saw the flyer on the seat and didn't bother answering; he just pulled out his handgun, shoved his hand through the open window and shot Johnny in the chest. He moved so quickly that Rose barely had time to scream before she saw the blood spraying out of Johnny's chest, his eyes wide in sudden terror as life exploded out of him.

"Oh my god, holy shit!" She yelled, flipping around to kick open the car door. She looked back once to see Johnny one last time, horrified, tears filling her eyes before she leaped out of the car.

Sheriff Tom spun the revolver in his hand and slammed it back into the holster on his belt like an old fashioned gunfighter. He snatched up the flyer from the seat of the car and stuffed it into his pocket before heading after Rose.

Rose kicked off the spiked heels she loved so much before her feet hit the ground and was off running toward the woods. She could hear Sheriff Tom pursuing her, his heavy footfalls like the beat of a drum in her head and though she ran as fast as she could, he was still rapidly gaining on her.

Within a few heartbeats he had caught up to her and reaching out while still running, grabbed her by the hair. He spun her around and flung her partially onto the grass in front of a thick tree.

"There's a new fuckin' sheriff in town, bitch!" He shouted in her face, holding her up tightly by the hair as he grabbed his pistol out of the holster.

Rose tried to fight him off but the sheriff slapped her hands away. In one quick movement he brought the gun down to her head and fired. A single jet of blood flew from the wound then it pulsed out with the final beats of her heart. Sheriff Tom released his hold on her and Rose crumbled to the ground, lifeless eyes staring at the night sky forevermore.

*****

A few hours later Sheriff Tom returned to the small cabin he was staying at. It looked more like an old barn from the outside, and it was hidden away from the public eye. Sheriff Tom had successfully managed to remain 'missing' for a year. He needed that, he needed to know what the repercussions of that night were going to be, and who, if anyone, would be blamed for it all. He needed to know that no one was going to point a finger at him and come hunting after him with a stint behind bars in mind for the 'missing' sheriff of Bernardsville.

He also had a new sense of power; the power that he got from reading, studying, the spell book he'd recovered from the Horowitz house. He'd learned a lot since 'Mary Horror Night', but he knew he had a long way to go because in a strange way he didn't feel 'complete' yet.

After cleaning up a bit to get any blood still remaining on his face and hands scrubbed off, he sat down in front of the fireplace, across from a small television, and pulled the 'Mary Horror Night' flyer out of his pocket. The flyer was printed on cheap paper and crackled in his hand as he smoothed it out and dropped it on the coffee table in front of him.

For a moment he could do nothing except stare at it intently.

"I'm so sick of this 'Mary Horror' bullshit!" He said angrily, slamming the top of the table with his hand. He let his hand fall on the spell book, which rested on the table close to him. "They're gonna fuckin' know who Sheriff Tom is from now on! That's who they're gonna be afraid of!" He felt a slight jolt from the book, sending a shiver of a spasm up his arm.

He'd gotten used to that, used to feeling the book empower him.

Sheriff Tom slipped a small photograph out of his top pocket and set it down on the coffee table in front of him. He leaned back in the old comfortable wooden chair, looking at it with sad longing.

It was a picture of Arleen Horowitz, not a recent picture, but she still looked much the same as she'd looked when he'd seen her around town just before her murder. 'Murdered,' he thought to himself, 'and I knew it was going to happen.'

"My sweet Arleen." He said, his voice a much softer rumble. "I wish you could be with me here right now. I should never have let them take you, so sorry." He stared off, hung his head and memories spooled together in his mind, a collage of events.

He remembered how it all began. It was a simple beginning; a phone call. Sheriff Tom tried not to wonder what would have happened had he not answered the phone that day.

But he could remember answering the phone. He recalled how he initially didn't like the sound of the mayors' voice, how he seemed to sound like a shyster so slick he could sell a screen door to a submarine.

"Well, I'm looking for a sheriff," Mayor Joe Grafton said with somewhat of a drawl. The sheriff could tell he was smoking a cigar just by the way he paused to inhale and exhale while speaking. "And from what I've been told, you're more than qualified. You're a good man too, and there would be a lot of money in it for you."

"I can certainly use a change of scenery." He remembered saying. A sheriff even back then, he still lived in Salem. At the time, he wanted to leave town just to walk away from the ache of his ended affair with Arleen Horowitz. Leaving the state was an added bonus because he'd never have to look back. Or so he thought. He had no idea the Horowitz family was also moving at the time.

He could see her, right in front of him, putting on her shoes while he tucked in his shirt after a nice long afternoon together. It was long before her death; many years in fact, at a time when having her in his life meant so much. The closeness, he needed it back then for so many reasons, just as he needed it now, or at least wanted it.

Then he realized that after becoming the sheriff of Bernardsville, he'd begun to work together on a 'special project' to turn the town into a tourist attraction with Mayor Grafton and a man named Jeff Horowitz, whom he found out was Arleen's husband.

He ran into Arleen a short time later, coming out of the municipal building.

"Hey, there's something I have to talk to you about-" he said, trying to get in front of her so he could talk. He put his hand on her arm hoping to slow her down, but she shoved it away.

"Just forget it Tom, it's been over for a long time." She said angrily. "I can't believe you followed me to New Jersey."

"Wait, I have to tell you something." He said futilely. She was gone before he could do anything else to try to stop her without it looking strange in public.

He wanted to tell her what her husband was doing with an underage girl. He wanted to tell her what Jeff and the mayor were planning.

It was his own part in it that had yet to be decided, but he was getting sucked into it faster than coke through a straw, and hoped that Arleen knowing could somehow fix everything, or at least prevent him from turning into a monster.

Things moved fast from there, too fast. The next thing he knew, he was getting his eye ripped out of his face and stabbed by a meat cleaver thrown at him by-

Mary.

Mary Horror.

He put the image of the young girl out of his head and let the anger regarding the entire situation build up inside him until he was totally enraged.

He stood abruptly, kicking back the chair and grabbing his shotgun from where it rested across the coffee table.

"They're all gonna pay," he hissed angrily through gritted teeth. "Every last one of them is gonna pay! I'm gonna run this fuckin' town!"

TWO

Earlier That Morning

JC opened the pub early on the anniversary of the 'Mary Horror Night' slayings. He couldn't sleep well, and didn't want to just kill time at home, so he went in early to catch the news and drink some strong coffee at the bar before anyone else came in.

He manually turned on the television over the middle section of the bar and took a seat, kicking back while the mid-morning local news came on.

"It's News 25 with Lonnie Anderson and Marilyn Stone," the narrator boomed as the screen showed Lonnie and Marilyn, both young and looking more like models than commentators, standing

back to back, smiling brightly. "With Chuck Marble, out in the field. It's time for action, it's time for News 25. Now we go to Chuck Marble." The narration ended abruptly, with Chuck Marble appearing on the screen with a big smile on his face.

"It's been nearly a year the brutal slayings by Mary Horror on 'Mary Horror Night'. "Mary Horror Night' itself has been indefinitely canceled by our new Mayor John Rockland." Marble turned toward the mayor, who was much older than Mayor Grafton, and after learning of how Mayor Grafton lost his life he also had an enormous bodyguard named Rocko. "We are now joined by the mayor. Mayor Rockland what do you plan to do to clean up the city?"

"I am happy to be a part of this great town of Bernardsville." Rockland had a very serious expression on his face and spoke quickly, but sounded more like Mel Brooks in an old movie. "I will clean up the mess left by the late Mayor Grafton, and put a stop to the 'Mary Horror' nonsense. We're going to get rid of 'Mary Horror Night' indefinitely. It attracts all sorts of undesirable people." The mayor proceeded to go on somewhat of a rant about said 'undesirables', using racial and homophobic slurs that luckily were

beeped out by the news station before hitting the air. News 25 had
learned from previous mistakes during live coverage to have a
slight delay in its broadcast. Chuck Marble nodded to the camera
and smiled when the mayor was finished and the audio resumed.
"Bernardsville has never had those kind of people hanging around
and I'm going to bring it back to the way it was."

"Well, there you have it, Mayor Rockland's plan to clean up
Bernardsville, starting with the ban of tonight's 'Mary Horror Night'
celebration. I'm sure that's going to raise quite a controversy
around town and I'll be covering it."

"You're quite an attractive young man." The mayor said to
Marble with a smile. "Y'know, I was thinking, maybe we should
discuss this further at one of the clubs in town. I hear the 'Manhole
Club' is quite good, why don't we head over there." He grabbed
Marble, who was grinning uncomfortably by the arm and started to
walk off, nodding to his bodyguard. "C'mon Rocko, let's get
going."

The screen went blank for a moment, and JC sat back at the bar
and cursed to himself.

"You'd think with all the money we pay for cable they'd have a decent news channel." He shook his head, annoyed. "What a bunch of idiots."

The screen came back to life, only it depicted Lonnie and Marilyn making out on the set. When they realized they were on the air both of them jumped up and tried to straighten their clothes and act like nothing odd had happened.

"Oh, well, um, it seems like the camera cut out." Lonnie struggled to say. "Sheriff Tom Walkers' body has still not been found, but there has been a group of hunters out scouring the wooded areas to look for his body, but no sign yet."

JC flicked off the news, frustrated at how inept people could be, especially when they have a job that puts them in the public eye. He got up and started to go through his regular routine, deciding that he would still take the night off in spite of how 'Mary Horror Night' had been cancelled.

*****

Billy and Jimmy had just gotten off work. They were driving into town listening to music, munching out on junk food and bopping to the music Billy had cranked up in the car. Several flyers for 'Mary Horror Night' littered the inside of the car.

As the song they are listening to ended, the DJ came on the radio. Billy can barely make out what's being said so he turns up the volume, stuffing a ketchup packet in his pocket while watching Jimmy tear into some French fries.

"And that was Crash Romeo with "Dial 'M' for Murder". DJ Red here. Now remember everyone; no celebrating 'Mary Horror Night' tonight, since our new illustrious Mayor Rockland has banned everyone from doing so. Mayor Rockland has gone out of town for the evening, but still insists that anyone caught celebrating will be arrested. In other news, wrestling manager Mike Johnson wins the Bernardsville Lottery, worth over two-hundred million dollars."

Billy turned down the radio and looked over at Jimmy, who was still munching on fries.

"Man, did ya hear that? Two-hundred million dollars. I could buy a million tacos from Taco Bell with that shit!" He said, sounding much more excited than he should have.

"Subway is way better." Jimmy said, looking at him with a crooked grin and a fry hanging out of his mouth.

Billy pulled the car over to the side of the road and stopped the engine. He took a moment to compose himself, then he smacked down on the steering wheel, still clearly frustrated.

"You've got to be fuckin' kidding me! You can't tell me that Subway is better than Taco Bell!" Billy looked at him with narrowed eyes, more than just annoyed. "Taco Bell has the Chalupa, the ninety-nine cent Chicken Burrito, and don't forget about the Big Box! I fuckin' love the Big Box! How can you say Subway is better?"

"I'm just sayin'." Jimmy was shaking his head at Billy. "They have the 'Five Dollar Footlong' and it's amazing. And look at Jared, he's a fuckin' stud!" Jimmy said, smiling.

"Well, Jared is a fuckin' stud." Billy nodded in agreement. "And, y'know, speakin' of studs, I thought of a way to impress the ladies tonight at the séance party!" He said with an evil grin.

"Let's fuck 'em!" Jimmy joked.

"No, we don't fuck 'em." Billy gestured to him in mock seriousness. "Get your head out of your ass Jimmy. I say we go to the library. Y'know they have copies of Mary's spells down in the basement, and we say some of the spells and we impress the ladies and can cuddle up next to 'em. Then we can fuck 'em. It'll be great!"

"Let's do it!" Jimmy smiled enthusiastically.

"Okay, now we can agree on something." Billy started the car again and put it in gear. "Let's go fuck some bitches and get some Taco Bell." He said, driving off.

"Are we gonna head straight for the library?" Jimmy asked, tossing the empty French fry container on the floor.

"No, first we have to pick up Kristen, then go to Eric's and Randall's place. We can stop at the library before we go to the party. Eric can probably get us down to the basement since his aunt works at the library."

"I still say she's dead." Jimmy laughed.

"Who?" Billy asked, squinting at him.

"Mary." Jimmy replied with a straight face.

"Oh, Christ! I guess you're right in a way this time. She was dead, and then she was alive, but still dead. Now she's the spirit that haunts the big yellow house."

Billy started making scary noises, which Jimmy didn't like. He turned up the radio to drown it out.

DJ Red here! We now turn over our airwaves to the internet broadcast of Horror Watch. DJ Red will be back within the hour!

Sitting in front of a camera in a small studio with music playing in the background was Roxsy Tyler. Roxsy is in her late teens, dressed in black, wearing a top hat and sporting face paint the makes her look like a cross between 'The Crow' and Alice Cooper. Her show, 'Horror Watch' was broadcasted simultaneously on the radio as well as online, where it could be viewed as well. The studio had a handful of people sitting as an audience in a row of folding chairs just out of camera view.

"Hey there guys and Gals, Roxsy Tyler here, comin' at you live from 88.7 FM and streaming live at 'Horror Watch TV'. And today on Horror Watch we're very excited to be talking to two vloggers that have seen Mary Horror first hand."

There was an uncomfortable silence, and the call of several crickets that must have lived somewhere in the studio.

"This is where you're supposed to applaud!" Roxsy barked angrily at her meager audience. "Applaud!" The small gathering applauded loudly, with Roxsy joining in herself with a fake smile on her face.

The camera pulled back to show two empty wooden chairs sitting next to Roxsy Tyler.

"Okay ladies and gentlemen, here they are, the Mary Horror vloggers!" She began clapping and looking at her audience again. "Clap, clap, clap. Applaud now."

After the two guests sat down, she stopped clapping and made a sweeping motion with her hands.

"Stop." She mumbled, to silence the clapping.

Roxsy looked at her two guests and smiled widely.

"Hey guys, can you tell our audience you names?" She asked, the smile remaining.

"Hi Roxsy, I'm Randy," he said smiling. He pointed at his partner sitting next to him with both of his index fingers. "And this is Mike."

Mike didn't move, sitting there with his hands clasped together in a white-knuckled grip. He put his head down and grinned nervously. The audience chuckled.

"He's a little bit shy." Randy confirmed, with a chuckle himself.

Randy looked as if he were in his twenty's, with long bleach blonde hair styled as if he were still living in the 80s less one can of hairspray. Mike, totally red-face embarrassed, resembled the typical geek; short hair, a perpetually wide-eyed nervous facial expression, and wearing a plaid button-up shirt. The only thing he lacked was a pocket-protector and glasses.

"So, can you tell me more of what you guys do? And what's your goal with these vlogs?" Roxsy asked.

"Well, first off, we love everything 'Mary Horror'," Randy sounded excited. He looked to Mike.

"Yeah," Mike sat there silently for a second then finally agreed; a glazed looking smile as he nodded nervously. Several members of the audience started laughing when he spoke.

"So we feel, that since there have been so many recent sightings of Mary Horror around Bernardsville that it would be our job to try to catch her on camera to show that she's not just a spirit in a house anymore." Randy, wound up, continued on, gesturing wildly with his hands. "She's much more than that and she's still out there roaming the streets of Bernardsville."

"But what about the new mayor and his recent ban on 'Mary Horror Night'?" She turned toward her audience and got them riled by mouthing 'boo' and showing two thumbs-down about it.

Mike, staring down at his hands, finally spoke up.

"Well, actually we're not trying to celebrate Mary's bloody rampage, we're just trying to prove that she's still out there." He said, still looking down, but grinning with the success of actually speaking up.

"Good luck guys." Roxsy said. She turned toward the camera. "This is Roxsy Tyler, and you're watching Horror Watch."

THREE

Marty Perkins was retired and living with his son in a small cabin in a wooded area of Bernardsville. He was a short man, just over five feet tall, and he looked like a cross between Buffalo Bill Cody, complete with an unruly handlebar mustache, and Charles Manson, with long wavy hair and wild eyes.

He enjoyed life in the woods. It was peaceful there, and he liked the quiet. The lack of noise allowed him to concentrate on one of his favorite pastimes; cleaning his guns.

That's exactly what he was doing when an unexpected guest arrived. He was working on an old handgun under a lamp.

"It's been a long time, Marty." The voice he heard was rough, deep and angry sounding, and he vaguely recognized it.

Startled, Marty jumped from his seat. He put the revolver down and took his glasses off to clean them, stepping forward. He felt slightly intimidated, but continued on toward a shadowy figure standing across the room.

"Is that you Tommy?" He asked, putting his glasses back on. He rubbed one side of his mustache nervously, squinting at the man standing in front of him, wondering how he slipped into the house without him hearing him come in.

When the man steps into the open and Marty sees who it is, he visibly relaxes, and takes a deep breath. Sheriff Tom faces him, looking grim and still carrying his shotgun. Marty glanced at the eye patch, the scars around it and sighed heavily.

"What the fuck happened to you?" He asked, taking his glasses off again to see him up close. "How'd you lose your eye?"

"Never mind." Sheriff Tom barked. "I need weapons, whatever you got."

"Sure Tommy, you know I have what you need, but, something doesn't seem right about you." He stepped forward until he was within a few feet of him. "Are you in some sort of trouble?"

"I'm fine." The sheriff's response was more of an angry sound then it was words.

"You wanna sit down-" before Marty could even finish his sentence Sheriff Tom took one long step forward and grabbed him by his shirt. He lifted Marty right off the ground and got directly in his face.

"Are you gonna help me or not Marty?" He said, gritting his teeth angrily at the older man.

"Sure, Tommy, sure, just take it easy." Marty said, panic rising in his throat like bile as his feet kicked the air.

Sheriff Tom put him down, and he stepped back a bit.

"It's been so hard lately, ever since Arleen got killed by that no good daughter-" Marty tried to say more but was abruptly cut off again by the sheriff.

"Just show me what you've got." He said, dismissing anything else the older man said. He could feel the rage building up inside him again, and just wanted to get what he needed to continue on.

Marty brought him over to the other side of the room where a rocking chair sat with a folded blanket on it. There was a small throw rug under it. Marty moved the chair out of the way and kicked the rug aside to expose a door in the floor itself. He lifted open the door, revealing boxes of guns and ammunition, with some of the boxes labeled 'U.S. Army'.

"This is all I've got." He said, waving a hand over the opening in the floor. "What are you gonna do with all of them?"

"I'm gonna take over this town and no one's gonna stop me, ya hear? Nobody!" He shouted with a clenched fist.

Marty backed off again, nearly afraid of him. He just watched as Sheriff Tom grabbed all the weapons and ammo, pulled them out of the opening in the floor and out to his car. When the door finally slammed behind him, Marty knew he wasn't going to be coming back inside to say 'goodbye'.

Suddenly, his son Ringo came into the room.

"What the fuck was that all about?" Ringo asked. He was an unshaven muscular man in his thirties, wearing a bandanna on his head and greasy work clothes. Like Sheriff Tom, he was also carrying a shotgun.

"It was Sheriff Tom. Ringo, you must not say a word about this to anyone!" Marty said sternly. "He is no longer human. He is a walking talking killing machine!   He's become some sort of monster! Anything he wants, you give to him! I don't want anything happening to you, do you hear me?"

"Okay, but if I see him again my military instincts are gonna kick in." Ringo said, holding the shotgun up close and pacing the room angrily.

"He's going to lead us to something I've wanted for years." Marty stared at him intently.

"Yeah?" Ringo asked, momentarily standing still. "What's that Dad?"

"A spell book. Your mother never let me get anywhere near it. Now with her and Mary both dead and gone, it's out there somewhere, and Sheriff Tom will lead us to it." Marty could feel his heart race at the thought of finally getting his hands on the book and the power it could grant him.

"I'll scour the woods and plan a stakeout of the town." Ringo said. "We need a plan of attack sir."

"Absolutely!" Marty said, saluting his son as he walked out of the room.

*****

Billy and Jimmy picked up Kristen, and made a quick stop at a liquor store for beer.

"You're not going to drink while you're driving right?" Kristen ran her hand through her hair, long and dark, to get it out of her face and narrowed her eyes at Billy, who had pulled out a beer while getting into the car.

Billy's eyes widened in mock surprise.

"You think I was going to drink this?" He asked, holding up the bottle. "I was just checking the expiration date. I forgot to in the store. You can't be too careful these days."

"Yeah, stale beer sucks." Jimmy confirmed, avoiding eye contact with the thin yet curvy passenger.

"Okay, well, let's get a move on then." She said, riding shotgun while Jimmy ducked in the back.

The trio got to Eric's apartment a few minutes later.

"We're gonna party tonight, Jimmy." Billy sang in a high voice, strutting down the hall with Jimmy and Kristen when they got inside Eric's apartment building.

They got to the door and Billy knocked loudly, still bopping to an imaginary beat in his head. They stood there waiting at the door for a few minutes before Kristen couldn't stay silent anymore.

"What the fuck is taking so long?" She said exasperated.

"He's probably flogging the dolphin in there." Billy said, turning back to her and laughing. "Maybe giving a stiffy and indian burn. I can't wait to party tonight!"

After a few more minutes passed Billy started to get annoyed.

"This is taking forever!" He mumbled.

"You sure we have the right room?" Jimmy asked.

"Yeah, I'll just knock again." He said, knocking harder that time.

Eric was in his bedroom, lying on his back throwing a soccer ball in the air and then catching it.

"Tonight is gonna be awesome Randall." He said, continuing to toss the ball in the air.

Randall was wearing a towel. She stuck her head out of the bathroom and smiled at him.

"I'll be right out." She said.

Eric thought he heard knocking.

"Is someone knocking?" He called out to Randall.

"I don't know, you better check." She replied, partially closing the bathroom door.

Eric got off the bed and tossed the ball aside, running a hand through his hair to make sure it was sticking up the way he wanted it to. He was a skinny guy and did his hair much the same as any standard punk rock singer from the 70s. He liked the music, but he liked the crazy lifestyles they had back then even more.

Just as he got to the door, Billy was inspired enough to try to open it on his own.

"Let me see if the door is unlocked." He turned to look back at Kristen. "He knew we were coming and all, so I think it would be okay."

Billy turned the knob and opened the door just as Eric was about to look through the peephole.

"This party's gonna rock." Billy said as the door slammed squarely into the side of his face.

"Ow! Son of a bitch!" Eric shouted while Billy, Jimmy and Kristen filed in. "Dude, what the fuck?" He said to Billy. "Hi Jimmy, Kristen." He held his face and nodded at his other two friends.

"Here's the beer." Billy shoved the bag into Eric, who took it and walked into the kitchen with it.

"Is Randall ready yet?" Kristen asked.

"She's in the shower." Eric said still complaining about his face hurting.

Billy immediately smiled when he heard him say that. He turned and slapped Jimmy on the shoulder.

"C'mere-" he said, wrapping an arm around Jimmy's neck and pulling him along.

"You really think they're gonna bring Mary back from the dead tonight?" Eric asked Kristen as they put the beer in the fridge.

"I don't know, maybe." Kristen grinned, not knowing what to really say. She'd really come along just to have some fun. The 'séance' was just an added bonus.

Billy pulled Jimmy away from them and toward the bedroom.

"Dude, Randall is in the shower." Billy looked at Jimmy urgently.

"Okay." Jimmy said, shrugging his shoulders and attempting to turn and walk away.

Billy grabbed him and turned him around so he could look him in the eye.

'Do you not know what that means?" Billy asked. "She's almost positively naked in there. Free tits, dude."

"Nice," Jimmy smiled. "Boobies."

"Let's go." Billy said.

He and Jimmy tip-toed through Eric's bedroom to the bathroom door. Billy got down on his knees in front of the door. It was open a crack, and he was able to see right through it when he was on all fours.

"I'll get down here." He said. "You get on top of me like we did in summer camp."

Jimmy laughs at the memory of a similar situation and complies. He can see the entire bathroom through the crack in the door.

Suddenly both of them see Randall come into view. She's wearing a light colored bra and dark blue thong.

"She's lookin' good tonight." He whispered.

"Yeah." Billy agreed. "Look at those tan lines."

Jimmy pulled a small piece of an Italian sub out of his jacket pocket and started eating it.

"I smell Italian sub." Billy sounded confused.

The two of them watch as she turns around and they see her perfectly shaped bare ass as she pulls up her pants. Their mouths are agape, and Jimmy falls off of Billy, landing hard on the floor and dropping his sandwich. Billy gets up and runs, with Jimmy a step behind him.

They got to the living room a second later to find Kristen and Eric sitting on the couch.

"So I hear this séance lady is one crazy horny bitch." Eric said to Kristen.

Billy's eyes bugged out when he heard that, thinking he'd been caught.

"What? Who's horny?" He said nervously. "I'm not horny. Jimmy are you horny?"

"What were you guys just doing?" Eric asked.

"Nothing." Billy said.

"Nothing." Jimmy echoed, munching on a pop tart that he had in his other pocket.

"Just making a phone call." Billy said. He looked directly at Eric. "Hey Eric, do you think you can get us down into the basement of the library? We need some copies of those spells. We want to impress the ladies tonight with some magic."

"Oh my god." Kristen agonized.

"You think you can get us in?" He asked again, ignoring Kristen.

"Yeah. Sounds good." Eric nodded. "I'll talk to my aunt when we get there. I think she's working tonight."

"Yes!" Billy said, spinning around and falling on the couch next to where Kristen was lying down. He bent low and tried to kiss her but Kristen held her hand up to push him away.

"Get off." She said totally annoyed.

Billy swung to the other side of the couch and banged into Jimmy who was already sitting there texting someone on his phone.

"You think Randall is going to get all scared tonight and cuddle up with me?" Eric asked Billy.

"Full moon." Jimmy said out loud, then whispered, "boobies pressed together."

"Jimmy thinks there's going to be a full moon tonight." Billy said with a chuckle.

"You guys are disgusting." Kristen shook her head. "I hope that bitch Rachael isn't going to be there. She's got to be 'Miss Perfect' all the time."

"I'm gonna plow Rachael." Jimmy said mocking her.

"Jimmy, dude, you are fuckin' whacked man, but I love ya!' Eric laughed.

Kristen rolled her eyes as Randall walked into the room.

Randall grabbed her purse and sat down on the coffee table, surprised at how quiet it was in the room.

"Hey guys." She said. Billy and Jimmy waved to her from the couch, both with silly smiles on their faces.

"When did Jimmy get into a zombie daze?" Kristen asked, watching Jimmy texting. She pulled a pair of black leather boots away from the side of the couch and started pulling them on.

"I don't know, he's been texting this fat girl all week. He says he loves her curves. I think he's in love or something." He made a funny face and looked mockingly at Jimmy, who kept texting. "You love that shit, don't you Jimmy?"

"C'mon, let's go." Eric said, getting up from the couch. "I'll text my aunt and tell her that we're going to meet her at the library." He said as they all headed out the door.

FOUR

"Tonight's vlog is going to be awesome!" Randy said to Mike. They were standing outside Roxsy Tyler's studio, and he couldn't have been more keyed up. "It's 'Mary Horror Night' and I know we can get something."

"Well, thanks to Roxsy's show, we're going to get even more hits to the website. Especially with this footage." He swung the video camera he was holding up toward Randy and grinned triumphantly.

"You're damn right. Now let's get started." Randy stepped back away from Mike and the camera.

Mike set the camera up, held it to his eye, got it focused and started to record the video.

"Jesus Christ, an old lady moves faster than you!" Randy complained. "Are you rolling yet?"

"Yes I'm rolling." Mike replied, slightly annoyed.

"Okay, it's 'Mary Horror Night' people, and very shortly we'll be going to Bernardsville, New Jersey, where it is forbidden to even be talking about Mary Horror. We will be documenting every step of our search for Mary Horror's spirit. We've already had several reports from local townspeople stating that they have seen her around town. And we will be the first to bring you images of Mary herself, so stay tuned ladies and gentlemen, because this is going to be an adventure that you won't soon forget. We'll be right back."

*****

The wooded area around what was commonly known in town to partiers as 'The Devil's Tree' was crowded with people of all ages by sundown. It was a secluded spot in the woods near a lake. Sheriff Tom arrived there just as the first fire was lit by a small group of friends already drinking beer. He stayed hidden in a cluster of trees that were overgrown with weeds around them, waiting for an opening, the perfect moment when he could spring into action.

Jo Jo, the gypsy that was supposed to be leading the séance, thought 'The Devil's Tree' would be a place of power where she would be able to contact Mary's spirit easily. She and her following had helped distribute the flyers.

As more people arrive, the entire scene looked like something out of a 60s revival, with people getting drunk and high, making out, or sneaking off to have sex.

Jo Jo saw them walk off and suddenly felt dirty. Before she got the séance started, she felt like she needed to be cleansed. Wearing a long dark red skirt and halter top, she scouted around the gathering for a male suitable for her needs. In her early thirties, Jo Jo preferred her men younger because they were strong and enduring, and she needed her man to have endurance if she hoped to be cleansed enough to perform a séance.

Jo Jo had a dark European look to her, with powerful yet soft features. Her hair was a mass of tight light brown curls spun around her slim oval shaped face. Her high cheekbones emphasized her eyes, which exuded emotion, or in the case of the evenings festivities, hunger.

After searching for a while and talking to a few men, she found what she was looking for dressed in black leather and wearing a black top hat. He looked to be in his early twenties.

"I need you to help me prepare for the séance. I'm Jo Jo."

"I'm Ron." He held up his beer in a mock toast, smiled and took a drink. Jo Jo simply grinned at him wickedly, took his hand and pulled him into the woods. He didn't argue with her.

Chris and Chrystal, a couple of young tourists that had gotten wind of "Mary Horror Night' from a flyer they'd seen while passing through town grinned to each other.

"She creeps me out little." Chris said, sipping on a beer. "I'm getting away from that Pluto lady." He said, backing closer to the trees behind them.

"Don't even worry about her." Chrystal said smiling. "Concentrate on shopping tomorrow. There are so many stores that I want to go to." She turned away from him but continued on absently. "I want to check out what's on sale, and I don't know, there might be a store closing too."

Sheriff Tom silently grabbed Chris from behind and pulled him back through the trees. He dragged him a short distance away and flung him down on the hard dirt.

Chris struggled to get to his feet, but the barrel of a gun was leveled at him and a split second later he felt his chest explode with the bullet that hit him.

By then Chrystal had turned back around and saw that he was gone.

"Chris?" She said, squinting in the darkness. "Where'd you go?"

Chrystal walked further into the woods and away from the party when she heard a gunshot in the distance. The other party goers heard it too, but joked about it being fireworks. Jo Jo had already begun her 'cleansing' by straddling Ron, and was riding him until he stopped at the sound of the gunfire.

"What was that?" he asked, breathlessly.

"Oh no, no, keep going, keep going," she said, digging her nails into his shoulders. "I feel dirty, I need to be cleansed," she gasped, continuing to ride him.

Mario and Dave, friends of Billy and Jimmy, were standing nearby drinking beer and watching the fire that burned by them when the shot rang out in the night.

"What is this? First a gunshot and now I'm hearing moaning?" Dave said, gesturing in the direction where Jo Jo and Ron were. "It's like two animals going at it."

"What, that?" Mario just shook his head knowingly. "It's probably just the night hunters, they're bound to be making strange noises if they're out here tonight."

"What the hell are the night hunters?" Dave asked, cracking open another beer.

"They hunt ghosts and zombies and ghoulish stuff. The mayor hired them to look for Sheriff Tom." Mario said.

"That's the most ridiculous thing I've ever fuckin' heard." Dave laughed, straightening his glasses afterward so he could continue to look around at all the girls around the fire, and possibly spot Billy and Jimmy when they showed up.

"Really?" Mario made a face at him. "After all we've been through you don't believe in ghosts?"

"Of course I do, I wouldn't be here if I didn't." Dave nodded.

"When are Eric and the rest of them supposed to be getting here?" Mario complained. "I want this thing to get started already. Where's that séance lady anyway?"

Jo Jo was smiling, and pulling up her pants at that very moment no more than fifteen yards away.

"The evil has left my body and now I am cleansed." She said dramatically, holding her hands up as if she were a surgeon that just scrubbed.

"Sure, whatever you say." Ron said confused. He straightened his hat and stood up. "I've got to piss."

Ron walked away from her without another word being said, and Jo Jo headed back in the direction of the crowd at the party new the 'Devil's Tree'. She still held her hands in the air and acted as if she were in some sort of trance, a glazed expression on her face.

Chrystal ran blindly into the woods after she heard the gunshot. She saw what looked like Chris by the light of the moon, and ran over to him. Sheriff Tom grabbed her before she could reach him and flung her down hard next to him.

Chrystal had the wind knocked out of her but looked at Chris, saw his dead eyes and put her arm over him while she started to shudder for breath and cry. She didn't see the sheriff pull the long, thin blade out of the sheath strapped to his leg; she just felt the jolt of agony and then sudden oblivion.

FIVE

The library wasn't very crowded by the time Billy pulled into a front parking space. Everyone squeezed out of his car and they went inside as a group.

Emma, Eric's younger sister was supposed to be going to the 'Mary Horror Night' séance with them was standing at the periodical counter near the front of the library. Unfortunately she wasn't alone. 'Smelly Tim', a guy none of them liked was there. It wasn't just the foul smell that followed him around all the time; it was his personality, or lack thereof that annoyed them all so very much.

"Oh hey guys." Emma said as she saw them walking in. "Look who I ran into." She made a sour face and gestured toward the guy standing next to her reading a newspaper.

"Oh hey Eric, what's up?" Tim said happily. "Are you guys going to that séance tonight?"

"Yeah, we're going right after this." He said, half smiling at Emma who was not pleased with the two talking at all.

"You think I can tag along?" Tim asked timidly.

Emma was mouthing the word 'No' repeatedly and when Eric looked back at the rest of his friends he could see that they didn't exactly want him to agree to Tim going with them either.

So Eric, to annoy everyone, said 'yes'.

"Yeah, sounds good." Eric smiled.

"Wow, thanks a lot." Tim said, following close behind as Eric led the group to where his aunt worked.

Billy came up at Eric from behind and swept an arm around his neck so he could speak to him quietly.

"Eric, are you fucking kidding me?" He asked. "Tim? You're gonna bring 'Smelly Tim' to the party?"

"We're just gonna give him a ride." Eric said, exasperated.

"Well, then let's just give everybody a ride." Billy said sarcastically. He stopped a kid walking in their direction and pulled him aside. "Escuse me sir," He said, over-politely, holding onto his should as if they were best friends. "You smell like balls, you want to come to the party with us?"

Eric pulled the guy away from Billy.

"You don't smell like balls, I'm sorry." Eric said pushing him along. "Will you please just stop it?" He said angrily to Billy. "Just wait over there and let me talk to Aunt Susan."

Eric's Aunt Susan was at the back counter helping someone check out some books. He heard her say, 'Back in two weeks' and knew that she was done with the patron so he approached her.

"Hey Aunt Susan." He said happily.

"Eric, what are you doing here?" She asked, tilting her head up slightly so she could see him in her glasses, which hung on the tip of her nose.

"Um, I kind of need a favor." He looked around to make sure that there was no one around listening. "Can you take my friends and I down to the basement? Y'know, to look at the Mary Horror stuff?"

"Right now?" She asked, eyebrows raised.

"Yeah, we've got to go to this séance thing." He replied.

"Hold on one second." She said, stepping away. When she came back she looked relieved. "Okay, we're a little slow, so I can take you immediately."

"Thanks!" He gave the group a 'thumbs up' and they were all following close behind.

*****

Dave and Mario had since gotten tired of waiting for Billy, Jimmy and the rest of the group to show, and in the meantime had picked up a couple of plastic 'Mary Horror Meat Cleavers' from a guy selling them near the fire across from them. They'd gotten into a heavy conversation about music when Jo Jo came walking out of the woods, heading straight for them.

"It's time to start. I am cleansed." She said dramatically, holding her arms up and staring up at the sky.

She came up on them so quickly they jumped.

"My friends aren't here yet." Mario said.

"We must start now, I am cleansed." She said, ignoring his words. "It is time!" She shouted.

"Whatever you say." Mario muttered with Dave agreeing more loudly.

"Yeah, apparently it's time." Dave had a difficult time keeping a straight face as he walked away to get another beer before the séance began.

Sheriff Tom studied the scene from his spot in the tree and laughed to himself.

"Bingo, Bitch!" He mumbled to himself, laughing at how she looked like an old lady calling out a win at a bingo game. He turned and walked back to where she and Ron had been earlier.

Ron was still standing by a tree pissing, his back turned to the sheriff. He could hear the guy sighing.

"Longest fuckin' piss, holy shit." Ron complained. "That gypsy bitch is one crazy lady. I better get myself checked out, who knows what she could have."

Sheriff Tom walked around to Ron's side and pulled out a long blade.

"I'll take care of it." He said, swinging the blade down so fast that Ron could only see a flash of silver before the pain hit him. He looked down and saw that his penis was gone, fallen somewhere in the grass below, and he was bleeding. The very sight of himself caused him to pass out.

Sheriff Tom stood there for a minute watching the man bleed out, then moved on, going back to the patch of woods where he'd been hiding.

*****

The library's halls leading down to the basement were all brick, and when they reached the door, Eric was surprised to see a 'Fallout Shelter' sign posted on it.

"Eric, do you realize that what we have in the basement are only copies, and not the originals?" His Aunt Susan asked when they reached the basement door.

"Ok." Eric nodded.

"It's not the original spell book." She took her glasses off and held the doorknob, waiting for a response.

"That's fine." He and the group agreed.

"Okay, I just wanted to make sure. You only have five minutes. I'll be waiting for you right out here." His Aunt Susan said, swinging the door open and letting the group past her.

"Done, thanks." He said when she walked away.

Billy held the door open for everyone, smiling as they passed him by. Jimmy was the last one. He smacked him in the arm with a grin and followed right behind him.

*****

Jo Jo stood in front of the tree, a small fire burning directly in front of her. A crowd of people had circled around her as she began the séance.

"We summon you Mary Horror." Her voice rose in volume as she stared up at the sky, eyes wide and determined. "Your soul is now free!"

A young partier, John, who was standing right next to Jo Jo looked over at his friend Rob and laughed.

"Dude, this bitch is whacked." He whispered, hand covering his mouth.

"Yeah, but look at how scared all the girls are. She's gonna get us all laid tonight!" Rob laughed. "We should have her at parties more often."

Gina, a curvy blonde, thinking Jo Jo was crazy and the entire séance was a waste of time, took her boyfriend Todd by the arm and led him away from the party goers.

"Let's get out of here for a while," she smiled, pulling him into the woods. "And have some real fun."

Sheriff Tom watches them leave from his vantage point.

The couple found a quiet spot next to a wooden fence away from the séance and start making out. Gina climbed on top on of Todd, and he suddenly grunts in pain.

"What's wrong?" Gina pulled away asking.

"Ah, I think I've been stabbed by Mary's cleaver." He smiled and pulled a plastic version of the cleaver out from under his back. "Ha! I'm just kidding with you baby. But I hope I get to stab you."

"You're so corny," Gina picked up the cleaver and smacked him with it, then begins to pick up where she left off.

Sheriff Tom stood in the shadows watching them. Gina sat up on Todd, and took her shirt off and things got even hotter as they started having sex right there in the dirt.

The sheriff approached them without making a sound, pulling out a long blade that looked like a cross between the knife he used on Chrystal earlier and a machete.

Todd, who, between the alcohol and Gina riding him, was in heaven. He was just lying back with his eyes closed when he heard a strange noise, like a boot crunching on some dead leaves. He thought that the last thing he needed was some screwball getting a video of him screwing Gina and posting it somewhere. He opened his eyes and wasn't sure he was really seeing what he was seeing. He thought he saw Sheriff Tom holding a long sharp looking blade, coming right at them.

But that couldn't be, because he'd been missing for a year already and everyone thought he was dead, especially Jimmy.

"Oh shit!" he shouted, trying to push Gina off.

"Shut up Todd," she said angrily, pushing him back down. "Just shut up and fuck me."

She slid him all the way inside her and start riding him fiercely again as the sheriff drew nearer. Todd kept trying to hold Gina back and get her off of him but he she was holding him down and he felt so good with her humping him like crazy that he couldn't find the words to shout before he saw the glint of the blade, and knew that what he was seeing was real.

Sheriff Tom grabbed Gina by her long blonde hair and pulled her head back. She looked up at him in terror and started to scream. He swung the blade low, as hard as he could. It sliced deeply into Gina just above her hips, stifling her scream. With another quick hack, the sheriff had cut her completely in half. He flung her upper body away and just stared at Todd, who had finally found a voice to shout with as blood began squirting out of the lower half of Gina's body.

He was covered in blood and felt Gina's insides clench up on him. He couldn't stop himself from coming just as Sheriff Tom raised the shotgun and pointed it at his head.

"What a way to go out Todd!" he said, shooting him in the head.

*****

Mario and Dave were standing by another fire with Ally, and Kim, their dates, laughing at how drunk some of the people had gotten as well as how crazy Jo Jo sounded.

"So where is Eric and everybody else anyway?" Mario asked. "I want to get this party started already."

"Party? This is so scary." Kim put her hand on his should, looking nervous.

"You really believe this Mary Horror stuff, huh?" He said to her.

"Well, when does anything like this ever happen around here?" She looked around nervously.

"Did any of you see where Todd and Gina went?" Ally asked, squinting in the darkness trying to find them.

"Hey, you know Gina," Mario laughed, "They're probably off fucking somewhere. They'll show up when they're done."

"Probably. Well, I just hope they get here before Eric and Randall and the rest of them get here, they're missing everything." Ally continued to look around to see if she could spot them somewhere.

SIX

The Horowitz house was still lit up at night, but it had been completely fenced off so that no one could get near the house. That didn't stop Molly from talking Chad into jumping the fence with her.

The pair had heard about 'Mary Horror Night' on the news and drove to Bernardsville with the hope of getting into the Horowitz house somehow. Chad really wasn't into it, but went along because he'd been trying to get in Molly's pants for weeks, and he hoped his persistence would eventually pay off.

Molly fiddled with the lock on the door using a hairpin and an old credit card.

"There's got to be a way in." She said, frustrated.

"Ever since Mayor Rockland took over this place has been nailed shut." Chad emphasized his point by smacking a fist into the door.

"I think, I got it!" Molly said triumphantly. She pushed the door open and turned back to look at Chad.

"Oh you've got it alright," he muttered under his breath while staring at her ass. "I mean, we've got to get in there, take some pictures, and then go back to my place and then you can use those pop rocks that we got at that candy shop, because this place is creeping me out-"

"Don't be a pussy Chad." Molly cut him off. She turned and pushed the front door open further but before she could walk in a shadow appeared in front of her. She looked at it strangely then suddenly the shadow flew into her, as if it had been absorbed by her, but in fact, it had possessed her.

It was Mary.

Molly suddenly had a cleaver in her hand; Mary's cleaver.

Chad saw the cleaver appear out of nowhere and started to sweat. He immediately went into panic mode when he saw her face as she turned around to face him. She looked the same, but her expression was one he'd never seen before. She looked evil, angry in a way he'd never seen. She raised the cleaver at him and he wanted to scream.

"You're scary!" He shouted, turning to run. "Get away from me with that thing!" He made it down the stairs before she threw the cleaver at him. He felt an explosion of pain between his shoulders and then tasted his own blood as he fell, pulling the cleaver out of his back as he coughed up blood. "That fucking bitch!" he said, not knowing they would be the last words he'd ever say.

*****

Eric had been going through a pile of photocopied spells when he came across one that really surprised him.

"Guys, listen to this." He stepped in the middle of the room so that the group was all around him. "It says that this will turn everybody into a member of the walking dead." Randall stood next to him with a nervous look on her face as he began to recite the spell. "Listen to this: 'May the living become the dead and eat the flesh that is bled.' It sounds so fucking dumb." He made a face and looked at Randall. "May the living become the dead and eat the flesh that is bled." He went around to the girls and made scary faces, moving his reaching out to them with his hands as if he's going to strangle them. "May the living become the dead and eat the flesh that is bled."

"Not when you say it like that." Tim actually looked scared. "That's some freaky shit, man."

"You smell like freaky shit," Billy said, looking at Tim.

Jimmy held his nose, grinning, and Kristen, who was standing next to him, put her hand over her mouth so she wouldn't laugh.

*****

After killing Todd and Gina, Sheriff Tom decided to spy on the rest of the séance, and when it was over and the gypsy séance leader was done, he would leap into the crowd, guns blazing. He saw them all standing around the fires getting drunk and listening to Jo Jo.

All of a sudden everyone fell to the ground. The sheriff looked around, totally confused as to what just happened.

*****

As Randy passed the 'Welcome to Bernardsville' sign he saw what looked like a zombie, standing right next to it.

"Holy shit!" he said looking back. "Mike, did you see that?"

"What the fuck was that?" Mike said, looking in the side view mirror.

"It looked like a zombie." Randy said, still looking back.

"No fuckin' way. Why would there be zombies in Bernardsville?" Mike shook his head in disbelief.

"Why would there be a killer spirit in Bernardsville? I don't know. Just get out the camera and start rolling."

Mike took the camera out and did just that.

"Oh my god, man, zombies." Randy said.

"Oh my god, zombies. Turn, man, turn." Mike said trying to get some footage from the car window.

He saw 'Smoochie' the dog, who had become somewhat of a celebrity in town because of the way his owner was killed, being walked. Mike filmed how the dog walker fell to the ground dead, and how 'Smoochie' rolled over and played dead beside him, until the dog walker stood up seconds later as a zombie.

"This is some crazy shit going on!" Mike's voice shuddered with fear.

"Mary's house is on this road." Randy slowed down so Mike could get better footage. "Look, there it is just up ahead." He point to the fenced off yard and the big yellow house that was lit up brightly.

"What the fuck is that?" Mike said filming a crowd of people crouched over a body, tearing at it like hungry animals. Their faces covered in blood and their hand clutching torn flesh.

"I don't believe my eyes." Randy said, sounding afraid.

"Pull over." Mike said.

"What about the zombies?" Randy asked.

"Just pull over." Mike demanded.

Randy pulled over near the Horowitz house. Mike got out and started to record the crowd of zombies tearing at their unknown victim and Randy stood nervously next to him.

"Get these zombies on film." He said to Mike.

"I know, I know," Mike said, already recording.

"Are you getting it?" he asked.

"Yes I'm getting it. It looks good." Mike replied.

Molly, still possessed by Mary Horror, was slowly coming up behind them. Randy and Mike were so overwhelmed by what they saw that they didn't even notice until it was too late and she was there right in front of them.

"Where's my book!" Molly shouted with Mary's voice.

Randy ran over to Mike and spun him around so he would start recording Molly and what she was saying.

Molly approached Mike and smacked away the camera. Before Mike could try to get away she had him by the throat and was lifting him off the ground. "Where's my book?" She swung the cleaver up, about to hack into him when Randy intervened.

"We don't have your book you dumb broad!" He shouted.

Molly flung Mike away but was tackled by Randy before she could come after him. He grabbed Mike and pulled him to his feet, taking hold of the camera and pushing Mike to the car.

"Hurry up, get in." he said, leaping through the car window and landing in the seat. He sped off before Molly had even gotten back on her feet again.

"I can't believe we actually got that on film." Randy said as they drove away. "Are you okay Mike?"

"My neck is killing me." He said, rubbing it. "She choked the shit out of me."

"Either there's another psycho ghost girl out there, or Mary Horror is in that girl's body." Randy looked at Mike and shook his head in disbelief.

"This doesn't make any sense." Mike said. "This girl just had the cleaver."

"There are zombies everywhere." Randy said nervously. "And now Mary is running out there as someone else? This is too much. So much for covering that séance that Billy's gonna be at."

"I just hope that everybody hasn't turned. We need to get somewhere safe." Mike was still rubbing his throat.

"Well I'm open for recommendations, tell me where to go." Randy gestured hopefully to Mike.

*****

"It says here that this spell was used to form an army to defeat the witch hunter." Eric said, flipping over another sheet of paper. "The witches would be able to control the walking dead. And here Rebecca says that one hunter's name was 'Walker'. He was a judge during all the Salem Witch Trials and he wanted all the witches dead."

Kristen imagined Sheriff Tom dressed as a Judge from that time period, complete with long white wig. She could see him taking part in the hanging of Rebecca, laughing as the poor woman was hanged. Absently, she put her hand over Billy's, for comfort, and Billy felt a chill go up his back, smiling like a kid on his first date.

"Guys, it's getting late." Randall stepped up next to Eric. "We should just get to the séance already."

"Yeah, yeah." Eric gathered the papers, folded them up and stuffed them in his pocket. "Time is up anyway."

The group went down the hall up the stairs with Eric leading the way. They rushed to the door where his Aunt Susan had left them. She was still standing there on the landing, with her back to them.

"We got what we needed," Eric tapped her on the shoulder. "Thanks, Aunt Susan."

She didn't respond, didn't even move.

"Aunt Susan?" Eric repeated, a little confused at her lack of response. He tapped her shoulder again and nearly jumped when she moved.

Slowly his Aunt Susan turned around to face them.

"Is she growling?" Billy whispered to Kristen.

There was no time for her to answer, because when Aunt Susan had turned completely around to face them, they all saw the gray skin and empty eyes. They saw the hungry expression on her face; and she was indeed growling at them.

As a group they screamed.

Eric backed up, totally freaked out by what he saw. Randall grabbed his shoulder and pulled him further away.

"Let's get the hell out of here!" She yelled, pulling him along as they all ran past his Aunt Susan, who had hissed at them but was moving too slowly to keep up with them.

The group ran toward an exit, passing a long window along the way. Billy did a double-take passing it, then stopped and went back to confirm what he thought he saw.

"Holy zombie tits!" He mumbled, dumbfounded as Jimmy approached.

"Com on Billy, we gotta get out of here." Jimmy said grabbing his arm. He let go when he saw Billy was silently pointing out the window, eyes wide in terror.

"What's going on?" Kristen said running back to them. "We have to get out of here."

The rest of the group followed her back, and they all see what Billy's been staring at outside. The entire area in the back of the library, Olcott Square was crowded with zombies.

The walking dead filled the streets, there was no escape.

"Holy shit!" Eric shouted. "What do we do?"

"I have no idea." Kristen said, looked up and down the street, seeing that there was no end to the shuffling dead people.

"The fucking zombies are everywhere." Emma said, looking over Eric's shoulder.

"What the hell is going on?" Kristen mumbled to Billy.

"I don't know, but we need guns, knives, anything that can keep us safe." Billy replied, turning to look back at the group.

"Let's get fuckin' guns!" Jimmy said.

"I know where we can get some!" Eric said, running back down to the basement. The group followed close behind. When they came to where his Aunt Susan was still roaming around he pushed her out of the way and they all passed by her again to return to the basement room, where there were lockers for employees. He went to a locker with his aunt's name on it.

"This is still a fallout shelter." Eric said, "So it would make sense to have a weapon or two here, but my Aunt was trying to get the library to start a room where historic guns could be put on display." He pulled open the locker door to reveal a lot more than a gun or two. There were more than enough pistols and rifles for each of them to have something. "Some of these might be old, but they all work. There might even be a couple of old grenades on the top shelf."

Emma pulled out a pistol and held it up to look through the site.

"Good thing our Aunt Susan is a gun-nut." Eric said, nodding at his sister. Emma nodded her head and cocked the revolver, flipping off the safety.

They cleared out the locker and handed all the guns out. Not all of them had ever fired a gun before, so they went around the library practicing on the zombies still inside the library with them. It got bloody, but it was effective.

Eric, trying to lighten the mood, found an oversized butterfly net and started to carry it around.

Billy and Jimmy wrapped bandannas around their heads, acting like they were trained hit men; even though neither one of them had ever fired a gun before.

*****

"A church Mike?" Randy complained. "Really? You brought us to a fuckin' church?"

"I mean, Virgin Mary, Mary Horror, I didn't know where else to go." He still looked scared, rubbing his throat.

"Well, this is stupid, let's get the fuck out of here." Randy said, turning to walk back to the car. "C'mon, let's blow this pop-stand."

"Dude, where are we going?" Mike asked when they got back to the car.

"I don't know but I can't believe you actually dragged me to a church. Where to next, a fuckin' 'Payless Shoes'?" Randy said sarcastically.

"Did you have any better ideas?" Mike asked, annoyed. "At least I tried."

Before Randy could respond a zombie jumped at him. The zombie pushed him back into a fence. "Watch the hair!" Randy said pointlessly. The zombie flung him down to the sidewalk and bent his head lower, jaws moving, teeth grinding together as he swung his head down to bite Randy's throat. "Mike! Jesus Christ Mike help me!" Randy tried to push the zombie away but he was too heavy. He could smell the rancid breath and gagged.

Mike saw a piece of rebar on the ground near a damaged part of the sidewalk. He grabbed it, ran over to where Randy was and threw it at the zombie.

His throw caught the creature in the chest, impaling it and knocking it off Randy. The creature still struggled to rise but it gave the pair what they needed: time.

They were able to get back in the car again and drive off.

SEVEN

"Why don't we just stay here until it all blows over." Tim said to the rest of the group. "It looks too dangerous out there."

They were all standing outside, their backs to the door of the library.

"We're all gonna get bit." Jimmy shook his head.

"We need to go to the séance to see if anyone else is infected." Eric said, holding his gun in one hand and carrying the butterfly net in the other.

"We're still going to the party?" Randall said wide-eyed. "Are you stupid?"

"We've gotta go, they're our friends." Emma confirmed what he brother said.

"Zombies should not fuck with me tonight." Kristen cocked her revolver.

"Let's go to my car." Billy said, making his voice deeper and nearly comical.

They formed a line, and moved forward into the parking lot. They spotted Billy's car and stopped dead. Zombies surrounded it.

"Billy, we can't go to your car." Eric pointed at the zombies, shaking his head.

"No, I guess we can't." Billy agreed. "There goes that idea."

"So much for an easy drive through town." Eric said.

"I guess we've got to walk through Olcott Square." Kristen said, holding her gun up. "Let's go."

Eric led the group, with Billy covering the rear. They slowly made their way down the street, weaving around the zombies.

"Why aren't they coming after us?" Tim asked.

"Just shut up and hope that it stays this way." Kristen said, urging him forward.

The zombies were a strange group themselves. Some of them looked and acted relatively normal. Some of them could even speak and were talking to each other while roaming up and down the street.

"This is some weird shit." Billy said, walking backwards to ensure that nothing came up behind them.

That was when he saw the homeless man. He couldn't remember his name, but he was like a town drunk; everyone knew who he was. The man seemed to be sleeping in an alley they were passing. A zombie stumbled on his legs, jarring him awake. He sat up abruptly and looked around in a panic.

"Zombies?" he said, yellow eyes bulging, oblivious to his own new gray complexion. "Zombies!" He jumped to his feet and ran through a crowd of them, passing Billy and his group. "Zombies! Run for your lives!"

"These don't look like normal zombies." Billy said, creeping up behind Eric as they navigated through a crowd of the walking dead.

"This is no time to rate the fucking things!" Kristen said as she narrowly avoided bumping into one.

They pass by a zombie nonchalantly eating a pizza outside a restaurant, as Chuck Marble reports from the square, no distinct differences in his mannerisms.

"It appears we have all turned into zombies. We are everywhere. We will eat you. More at eleven. Back to you in the studio, Lonnie." Marble looked nearly green, and there was blood smeared on his face.

Back at the studio, Lonnie and Marilyn report as zombies.

"Thanks Chuck." Lonnie says into the camera, look pale and grayish. "It even appears that zombies are having sex on the streets in the square."

"Is that a fact?" Marilyn asked, grinning wicked into view.

"Let's cut to the clip." Lonnie says, disinterested.

The clip shows two zombies on top of each other, and though it seems they're having sex, they're actually eating each other flesh.

The clip ends and the camera flashes back to the studio.

"People are really making the most out of this outbreak alright." Marilyn says with a sexy smile.

"They certainly are." Lonnie pulls out someone's severed arm and begins to gnaw on it.

Back at the square, Eric stopped the group.

"Alright, we make it up the alley, down the street, pass 'Old Man Millies' and then we can book it to Twin Lakes." He said to them. "Girls, stay behind the men, we'll protect you."

"Um, excuse me," Kristen said angrily. "We can take care of ourselves, thank you very much."

"Yeah, we've got this." Randall agreed.

The two of the cocked their guns, and Billy tried to imitate what they did, but couldn't. Kristen saw him having trouble and ended up cocking his gun for him, shaking her head.

They made it most of the way down the alley without incident, until they came to a dumpster where a zombie was leaning against a wall. The dead man was digging his hand into some hapless woman's head, pulling out bits of brain and eating it, all the while making growling sounds.

They all stopped dead in their tracks.

"Oh my god I think I'm gonna puke!" Kristen said, backing away from the scene.

"That's disgusting." Randall said, following Kristen.

"Ew, he's eating brains." Emma said with a hand over her mouth to prevent her from puking.

The zombie heard them and turned around to face them. He dropped his current meal and started to shuffle toward them.

"Run!" Eric said, leading them all back the way they came.

Only Jimmy stayed behind. He pulled the one grenade he snatched up from the locker out of his pocket and held it in his hand like a baseball. As the zombie approached he pulled the pin and let the zombie grab his arm. It pulled on his hand, trying to get it to his mouth, which was when Jimmy let go of the grenade and jumped back.

The zombie held the grenade up to his face, fascinated, and then put it up to his mouth and tried to bite it. The explosion that happened a second later sent nearly the entire upper half of his body raining on Jimmy and the rest of the alley. The group could only watch in amazement at Jimmy's heroic act as blood and fleshed rained in the alley.

"You were great." Billy said, patting Jimmy on the back.

"Yeah, you were awesome." Tim blurted out, looking over what was left of the zombie.

"He's dead!" Jimmy grinned.

"You can say that again." Billy laughed.

"I can't believe you guy are still doing that 'She's dead' thing." Kristen said, flustered.

They moved on in silence, even more wary than before of the dangers they faced.

*****

Mayor Rockland was making his way to his hotel room where he made a quick call to Chuck Marble.

"Yeah Lance, I just can't seem to keep you out of my mind." He said excitedly. "In fact, that night at the 'Manhole Club' you were hot. You were so hot."

"My name is Chuck, not Lance." Chuck replied, still at Olcott Square. "I want to eat you."

"Yeah, I'm ready to be eaten." Rockland responded. "I've washed myself down there, don't worry, don't worry."

"Uh huh." Chuck said.

"Yeah, Lance, take me to the stars!" He said, grinning. Suddenly he looked down the hall and saw a female zombie stepping out of a room. She spotted him immediately and ran at him, snarling. "Holy zombie fun pillows!" He screamed as the zombie grabbed him and bit into his throat.

*****

The group had made it through the alley and was passing through a parking lot when Billy saw it and stopped, in awe.

It was a Delorean.

The doors were open, and when Billy looked inside, he was shocked to find that the keys were still inside it.

"It's totally fucking awesome!" Billy looks at the car glazed with a smile. "I totally have a nerd boner right now."

"You guys are so funckin' stupid." Emma says while pointing her gun at a couple of oncoming zombies, but none of them seemed to notice the group.

"Let's get in the car." Billy said, running over to the driver's side.

*****

Sheriff Tom watched as all the people that dropped to the ground just moments ago slowly rise up. He could see the changes in their complexions by the light of the fire. The way they moved, the jerky spasm kind of movements, and the lashing out at one another, it all told him exactly what happened. He just wasn't sure why it happened, or how for that matter.

The sheriff took a cigar out of his pocket, and some matches. He struck a match on his eye patch and lit his cigar with it. Feeling relaxed, in spite of the apparent danger, he lifted his leg up to rest his foot on a large rock in front of him and cocks his rifle, puffing on the cigar like a new father.

"Time to fuck up some zombies!" He snarled, charging toward a bunch of them. He blows several of their heads off, and stabs those that were left. One by one they go down, and the woods become a bloodbath.

"I fucking hate zombies!" He shouts, continuing to fire on more of them as they try to surround him.

The sheriff is high on the thrill of killing, thoroughly enjoying himself. He allows one of them to get close and hacks off his arm. The body falls, and Sheriff Tom blows his head off with his shotgun, tossing the arm away as blood and gore splash up at him. Another zombie was coming up on his right side. He raised his pistol without even looking, and fired one round, blowing off half the dead girls head.

"I'm gonna kill every last one of you fuckers!" He grumbles, firing at several more.

EIGHT

"Wow Jimmy, a Delorean." Billy said to Jimmy. They're both sitting in the car, but Billy's eyes are bugged out and he's got a grin on his face as if he just won the lottery. "We can go back in time and forget about the zombies."

"Let's go back in time, bitch." Jimmy said, half-serious.

"Fuck yeah! What do you think Eric?" he said, looking at Eric who was standing right by him outside the car.

"We're all not going to fit in there." He said in frustration. "Get out of the car and let's find something bigger."

"Ah man, he said no Jimmy," Billy frowns, "I guess we gotta get out."

"C'mon," Eric said, leading them away from the Delorean. "Let's get something bigger."

They all walked through the parking lot searching around but still very much on their guard. Eventually, Eric saw a Volkswagen Van. It was dark blue and looked like it was lost in the sixties, with interior lights that were still on and a string of black lights around the ceiling on the inside of the vehicle.

"That's it. There's our ride." Eric said running over to it. The rest of the group followed, with Randall calling 'shotgun'.

Their clothes and eyes glowed eerily because of the black lights.

"Hey, they left us the keys." Eric smiled.

"I bet a lot of cars have been abandoned like that with everyone just turning into zombies." Randall said.

The engine started right up, and Eric drove out of the lot, taking to the streets and heading to Twin Lakes.

"Let's see if there's anything on the radio about what's going on." Eric flicked it on and turned the volume up.

"DJ Red here, more like DJ dead. It seems like everyone is zombified! The zombie apocalypse is upon us. We've been informed that there will be a brain buffet at Olcott Square in five minutes. I've got dibs on the medulla oblongata. More after this next song, brought to you by Zumba for Zombies, Come on down to the Z."

"What the fuck! Talking zombies!" Tim was more than frustrated; nothing made sense to him and he was terrified that he was going to get bitten and turn into one himself.

"This is weird," Emma said, "I wonder why some of the zombies are almost normal and why others just want to eat people."

"Who knows," Kristen looked at her sternly, "We just have to survive somehow, and maybe if we make it through this, we'll find out later."

Suddenly, the van slammed into a zombie before Eric could steer out of the way.

"Watch out!" Randall shouted to him.

"They're everywhere." Eric yelled, trying to weave a path around them. Eventually seeing how many there were on the road, he gave up and started to drive right through them. The van wasn't his and he didn't care if it got dented up or not.

"Plow those fuckers down Eric!" Billy shouted when he hit a few more.

"Kill 'em." Jimmy said, texting on his phone again.

"There's Rachael!" Kristen yelled, pointing at one of them. "Plow that bitch down!"

"I'll plow her." Jimmy said not even looking up from his phone.

Rachael slammed face-first into the windshield of the van.

"Die Bitch! Die bitch!" Emma said as the zombie slid off the front of the van, face leaving a thick gory smear on the windshield.

"This is awesome!" Billy smiled.

Tim was totally grossed out, falling against Billy when the van was rocked by a zombie flying into it.

"Get off me, you smell." He said, while Jimmy just grinned.

"I told you I was going to plow Rachael." He smirked at Billy for a second and then continued on with his texting.

A short time later, after barreling over several more of the walking dead, Eric passed the Twin Rivers sign.

"I see Twin Lakes!" He pointed at the sign triumphantly.

They parked on a deserted road near some docks. A female zombie started to come at the from the water, but Emma quickly shot her down.

They made it into the woods, and were heading toward the 'Devils' Tree' when Eric stopped short.

"There's shit everywhere." He said looking down.

"There's zombies everywhere!" His sister chimed in.

"I think zombies are shitting everywhere." Billy snickered.

"Alright, let's go!" Eric said, running down the path that would lead them to the tree where the séance was supposed to be taking place.

The trail they followed was full of zombies. As a group they took down as many as they could, and kept on going, hoping that at least some of their friends were still at the séance and not zombies.

*****

Jo Jo, now a zombie, but still partially in control of herself, flipped out, when she saw that people, zombies or not, were being gunned down by the sheriff. Shrieking, she angrily tried to attack Sheriff Tom.

The two circled each other, with Jo Jo bobbing and weaving as if she were drunk and in a boxing match. Sheriff Tom reached out with lightning speed and grabbed her by the hair, flipping her over and onto the ground. He stepped on her back and twisted her head in an impossible direction. There was an audible 'snap' and her neck was broken. The sheriff let go and her head hit the ground as he laughed.

"Crazy bitch!" he shouted, immediately firing at more of them.

As they drew closer to him he began using his knife more often, slashing and stabbing, and at one point a large female zombie got so close to him that he was able to hack through her ribs and tear her heart out with his free hand.

As their numbers dwindled, Sheriff Tom took out his shotgun again to finish off the last of them near the fire. He saw that one of them couldn't have been more than twelve years old.

"Who brings a kid to a séance?" he said aloud.

Satisfied that he was safe at the moment, he flipped the shotgun over his shoulder and into a holster he had strapped there, still holding on to one of his pistols.

A young couple, zombies that were in the process of getting high sat on a tree stump a few feet away from him. The man and woman started clapping. They both stood up and walked toward the sheriff, who was surprised to see that he missed blowing them away.

The female started laughing hysterically, taking a hit off a thick joint and pointing at the sheriff. She handed the joint to the man and he puffed on it hungrily, eyes rolling back in his head.

"You fuckin' killed it!" She said to the sheriff, still laughing and clapping her hands and they walked closer to him.

The pair were giggling uncontrollable because they were hallucinating, seeing Sheriff Tom dressed as a ballerina, wearing a pink tutu, with oversized pink glasses on, dancing on his toes with his hands over his head.

"Touché sheriff," the man said, stepping away to attempt to dance on his toes. "I can do that shit too." He fell over in the attempt, laughing hysterically.

Sheriff Tom slid out his shotgun and walked to where the man had fallen over. The man was still laughing because all he could see was the sheriff spinning around as a ballerina. Sheriff Tom stabbed him in the chest with the shotgun. As he pulls the gun free, he took a taser out of his pocket and slammed it into the girls' throat.

The girl stops laughing and starts to shudder and shake, the skin on her throat burning. Sheriff Tom holds the taser to her throat until her eyes roll back in her head and smoke is visible from her head, then he shoves her aside.

"Ha, Kentucky fried zombies." He chuckled. "The sweet smell of victory."

Suddenly, he hears Eric and the rest of the group approaching in the woods. He twists around, running back to his hiding place from earlier in the evening, but the spell book falls out of the strap he had connected to his belt. It lands near the fire, and he doesn't even notice that it's gone.

"What the fuck happened?" Eric asked when they reached the clearing.

"Everyone's fucking dead!" Emma said, looking around at all the bodies and body parts strewn about.

"It looks like after my mom makes meatloaf." Randall made a sour face.

"Your mom's meatloaf sucks." Kristen said.

Billy walked over to a female zombie. He lifted her arm so he could see her face, which was covered in blood, and looked up at Jimmy.

"Looks like you in the morning Jimmy." He laughed.

"Fuck you Billy." Jimmy gave him the finger.

Suddenly the zombie opened her eyes, and the hand that Billy held clutched for his throat. It grabbed him and started pulling him down, toward her open mouth.

Jimmy pulled out his gun and shot her in the heard before she could take a bite out of Billy's throat.

"Die motherfucker!" Jimmy said mechanically.

"Jesus Christ Jimmy, I didn't realize that you had any balls." Emma said after watching him.

"Let's check for survivors." Eric said, looking around.

They all split up and started looking over the bodies.

"Who the fuck brings a kid to a séance?" Billy said, seeing the same young boy that Sheriff Tom had earlier.

"Holy shit!" Eric said, stopping in his tracks. He crouched down. "Check this out."

The group formed a circle around him.

"What is it?" Randall asked.

"That's Mary Horror's spell book!" Kristen said.

"What do you think the spell book is doing out here?" Emma asked.

Lurking in the trees behind them, Sheriff Tom slams his fist in the air. "My Book!" He whispers harshly.

"I don't know Emma, what do you think?" Eric asked.

"The sheriff?" Randall said.

"No way." Billy laughed. "I'm not dealing with that nut sack."

"The sheriff has been missing, and so has the book." Kristen insisted. "He must have taken the spell book and fled. He has to be out here somewhere. He must be the one who killed all these zombies."

"That's kind of a crazy scenario, don't you think?" Eric said doubtfully.

"And zombies in Bernardsville isn't a crazy scenario?" Tim offered. "Right?"

"Alright. But then why would the sheriff take the book and then hide for a year." Eric asked. "It doesn't make sense."

"It kinda does." Billy said. "I mean it does look like the real thing, and I've never seen anything like it before. Jimmy and I did see the sheriff a year ago with the book."

"He could still be around here." Emma suggested. "I always hear stories about him living in the woods with some old man."

"You think it could be Mary?" Kristen asked. "She's been seen around town."

"It could be." Randall said. She walked over to one of the nearest bodies and bent over it, studying the wound in its head.

"Ah, you sure you want to do that Randal." Billy said. He was standing next to Jimmy and Eric. The three of them were looking at Randall's ass in her tight jeans. Jimmy took a picture of it with the camera in his phone.

"It's okay Billy. The way these zombies were killed, it couldn't have been Mary. They were killed with a shotgun." She heard Jimmy's camera go off and turned around to look at the three guys. "Did you get a good look Billy? Like you did at the apartment?"

"What?" Eric asked, annoyed.

"What? No. Mariachi, the zombies are calling me." Billy said, clearly embarrassed. He walked away hoping that was the last he'd hear of it.

There was an echo of gunfire, and Billy made a bee-line directly for Jimmy, standing close to him.

"What the hell was that?" He asked.

"The sheriff." Tim said casually. "It has to be him."

"We're fucked." Jimmy said absently, still typing into his phone

"Are you still texting that girl?" Billy asked Jimmy, fingers still dancing across the keys of his phone.

"Yeah!" He replied happily. "Day and night, day and night."

"Wait a minute. She's not a zombie?" Eric asked, looking at his phone.

"No, she lives twenty-minutes away." Jimmy grinned.

"Maybe only the area is infected." Kristen said.

"Guys, I think it's time we get help." Tim declared.

"Who's gonna help us Tim, the fuckin' zombies?" Eric shouted at him.

"Oh zombies please help us." Emma joked.

"If there's people that are two miles away that are fine, than we could definitely get help." Tim pointed out.

"Then go on smelly, get," Billy made a pushing gesture with his hands, "get the hell out of here."

"This smell is going to be the smell of victory when I return with help." Tim turned and left the group, heading into the woods. "Tim, out," he crossed his hands in front of his face.

"That guy is a fuckin' idiot." Billy grunted.

"You didn't have to do that Billy." Eric, irritated, stared at him.

"Why not? He smells like balls." Billy chuckled.

"You smell like balls soup." Eric stammered.

"That's potpourri, you got a problem?" Billy looked at him angrily.

"Don't you have some friends out of town that you can call?" Eric thought a second. "What about that kid Randy? Isn't he obsessed with all things Mary Horror, including that spell book?"

"Yeah Randy's obsessed with all that shit." He pulled out his phone. "Well, let me see what I can do. I'll make some calls."

Billy stepped away from the rest of the group and started making calls. He had several numbers on speed dial and just started hitting them. The first number was labeled 'Murdock'. For a minute he couldn't remember who it was then he grinned and hoped the guy would answer.

"Hey Murdock, do you still do that thing called the 'B Team' or something?" Billy sounded hopeful when Murdock answered his phone.

"That's the 'A-Team'." Dwight Schultz replied, signing autographs at a convention.

"Oh, the 'A-Team'."

"Don't you know anything about show business?" Dwight sounded slightly annoyed. "I'm finished with that stuff, alright?"

"Alright, thanks anyway." Billy mumbled under his breath, "Well, it was worth a shot."

*****

Eric flipped through the pages of the spell book, when Emma backed further away from them. The rest of the group followed her and Billy was no longer in sight.

"Ew, that was nasty." She said totally grossed out. "I just want to get away from all those zombies."

"Y'know, this is our fault." Eric sounded nervous. "We said those spells in the basement. We were in that old fallout shelter."

"Is that why we're not infected?" Kristen asked. "Maybe we should find a place and wait this out until morning like Tim suggested."

"There has to be a way to reverse the spell, and get rid of the sheriff and all these zombies." Randall said to the group. "I think we should bring the book back to Mary's house."

*****

While they debated what to do, Billy finally got through to someone else.

"Hey Butch," He tried to sound happy and casual, not wanting to bring the subject of zombies or needing help yet. "How're you doing buddy? Weren't you involved in something called 'monster' or something?"

"That was 'The Munsters'." Butch Patrick replied, signing autographs a few tables down from Dwight Schultz.

"Just hang up on him!" Dwight shouted to Butch. "That clown just called me too. He seems to think we're really the characters we played on television."

"Oh Christ! How do all these whacky people get our phone numbers?" Butch clicked his phone off and continued to sign autographs.

The phone went dead, but Billy wasn't surprised. He had one more call to make, but he knew it would pan out, unlike the others. He thought about the rest of the group for a minute, hoping that he didn't lose anymore of his friends. The idea of any of them dying brought a chill up his spine.

*****

"We don't even know if the sheriff is a zombie, or what happened to him." Eric sounded even more nervous. He didn't want to go to Mary's house, it was freaky enough to him just being where he was surrounded by dead bodies.

"That's true," Randall agreed, "but there has to be a way to get rid of all this crap."

"I think I gotta go take a shit." Jimmy mumbled, lumbering off into the woods. No one noticed that he'd left.

"It says here that the book has to be in the rightful owners hands." Eric pointed to the spot on the page.

"Which is Mary." Kristen said.

"It must live with the spirit of the owner for things to be right." Eric read.

"So we go to the house." Randall said sternly.

"There have been sightings of Mary." Eric pointed out. "Maybe they raised her spirit just in time to help us. If Billy can get a hold of Randy, maybe we can find out what to do. Hey, where did Jimmy go?"

"Who knows?" Randall looked around, "Those idiots are always lost. He probably ran off to go text that girl again."

"We have to find them." Eric sounded determined. "We have a better chance of getting through Olcott with them, and we have to see if Billy got in touch with Randy."

"But the sheriff is still out there." Randall said, frustrated.

"I think I see him." Kristen squinted, looking past them.

"I don't see shit." Eric declared. "Don't worry though, we have ammo."

"Don't fuckin' move!" Ringo shouted pointing his shotgun directly at Eric.

"Sheriff Tom!" Eric yelled in a high pitch voice, terrified.

In shock, the group threw their hands in the air, looking at the shotgun and not making a sound.

"I'm not that crazy asshole! I did see him earlier though!" Ringo shouted at them. "He's one fucked up dude!"

NINE

Tim held his gun close as he made his way through the woods. The tree-cover blocked most of the starlight, and even though it was a full moon he could barely see in front of himself.

Suddenly he heard laughter all around him. It was a deep, evil sounding laugh that he could only compare to something he'd hear in a horror movie like 'The Exorcist'. He was already afraid just by being out in the woods, but after hearing the laughter he wanted to run screaming. The only thing keeping him merely standing was the idea that it could be the guys messing with him.

"Eric!" He called out. "Billy this isn't funny, don't be a dick!"

He tried to look around, still not moving from the spot he was in.

"Why did I leave the group?" He mumbled.

The laughter got louder, and seemed to be coming from behind him, but before he could turn around Sheriff Tom ran up behind him and lifted him off the ground.

The sheriff carried Tim, kicking and screaming to the side of the bath he was walking to where a wire fence had been. One of the metal posts was still sticking out of the ground. Sheriff Tom lifted Tim higher and slammed him down on it, impaling him.

Blood poured out of Tim's mouth as he slid all the way down the post until his back finally touched the ground. He tried to scream but only succeeded in making a loud gurgling sound before he died.

Sheriff Tom just stood there, laughing and watching him die. When the blood stopped flowing and Tim's eyes were empty and dead, he turned and headed back to where the rest of the group was.

"He smelled like shit!" The sheriff muttered, still laughing.

*****

"I'm Ringo, and I live in these woods." Ringo waved his gun at them. "And you're all trespassing."

"Sheriff Tom, you saw him." Eric's voice trembled slightly. "I knew he was still alive."

"He's not right in the head." He lowered his gun slightly. "What the fuck are you kids doing here?"

"We just came to get the spell book because everyone's a zombie." Eric stuttered. "We just need to reverse the spell, but we have to get through Olcott Square."

Ringo started to laugh.

"I've been pickin' off zombies in these woods all night, and you think you're going walk through Olcott Square with these fuckin' brownies?" He swept his gun across where the girls stood.

"That's the only choice we have." Randal said calmly.

"Roger that." Ringo said as he eyed up Randall. "Who set off this spell anyway?" He grabbed the front of Eric's shirt. "Was it you? Because you're the only other normal humans that I've seen all night."

"Um," Eric couldn't find his voice.

"Eric did it!" Kristen was standing next to him, and pointed right at him when she said it.

"Kristen-" He whispered harshly at her.

"But you did!" She smirked at him.

"Okay, Okay, yeah, I did, but we're gonna fix it." He said to Ringo in a panic.

Ringo shook his head, frustrated. He paced in front of Eric as if contemplating his next move.

"Why aren't you a zombie?" Eric asked him.

"I was in the basement when you guys set off the spell. I've been in there since I got back from the war. Me and Marty turned it into a bomb shelter, because you never know when someone is going to try to blow your ass up, or a bunch of fuckin' idiots are going to turn the entire town into zombies!"

"That's why we're not zombies too." Eric sputtered nervously. "We were in the library, in the basement, which is an old bomb shelter for the town."

"Okay, you can all put your hands down. I'll help you guys." He looked directly at Eric. "So what's the plan?"

"We have to get this book back to Mary's house. The whole spell will be erased there." Even though Ringo was now on their side, Eric could still feel his heart pounding in his chest like it wanted to jump out and run away from home.

"Alright, then let's go." Ringo headed off into the woods, with Eric and the rest of the group following him.

"I think he's kind of hot," Emma whispered to Randall while they were trying to keep up.

A zombie shuffled quickly toward the group. His face was a torn up bloody mess, his boney fingers clutching for them. Ringo lifted his shotgun up with one hand and blew his head off.

*****

"Randy, I'm so glad you're not a zombie!" Relief washed over Billy.

"Dude, Billy, we saw Mary!" Randy leaned back in his car seat glad to hear another human voice.

"What?"

"Mike and I were over in Chester, starting out the 'Mary Horror Sightings' video, and when we entered Bernardsville, there were all these zombies running around. So we took out the camera and started filming. Then, when we got near Mary's house, we saw this woman walking around out there. I'm pretty sure that Mary entered her body. No, I'm positive it's her!"

"Ah, you've got to be fucking kidding me!" Billy shook his head in disbelief and frustration.

"I really think it's her."

"Randy, I don't know how much more I can take of this shit!" Billy kicked the dirt angrily. "We heard gunshots before. We think the sheriff's in the woods."

"I think Mary was looking for her book." Randy said.

"We have the book!"

"What? How'd you get that?" Randy's eyes went wide and he looked over to Mike and saw him do a double take.

"We found it in the woods. I think it's the real one."

"Okay, listen. What you have to do is return the spell book to Mary's house. Her spirit still dwells there, and since she's the rightful owner, once she has the book back, everything should go back to normal. Someone must have taken it and that's why all this has been happening."

*****

"I saw you staring at him." Emma laughed. "You totally want Billy's shit." She was a couple steps behind Kristen, and busting on her.

"Absolutely not!" Kristen's response was half-hearted, but she tried to sound firm about it. "He's such a pain in the ass. He talks too much, always wears that stupid jacket-" She continued on with her list of Billy's character flaws, but Emma wasn't listening. She knew the real deal when she saw it.

The pair of them were the last in the group. Sheriff Tom had been following them since they left the séance area. When he saw Emma fall slightly behind Kristen, he silently crept up and grabbed her, wrapping a hand over her mouth and lifting her off the ground. Emma tried to scream while struggling, but all she succeeded in doing was drop her pistol.

No one would know she was missing until they looked for her.

When the sheriff was sure they were far enough away, he tossed Emma onto the ground directly in front of a tree. He had visions of pinning her to it with the long blade he slipped out into the open air. Emma saw the edge reflect light at her and started crying.

"No! Please stop!" She was so shocked by her unexpected abduction that she couldn't catch her breath of stand.

Sheriff Tom approached her slowly. He liked seeing the terror in her eyes. Emma started to get angry for letting herself be such a target. She forced herself to take a deep breath and picked up a rock. Rising to a crouch, she threw the rock as hard as she could at the sheriff, pegging him on the side of his head.

"Bitch!" He grunted, getting closer to her in spite of the rock.

That was when he noticed the zombies. There were quite a few of them and they were closing in fast.

"Fuckin' zombies!" He snarled. He grabbed Emma by the throat and lifted her to a standing position, holding the knife up to her throat. "Now don't you move! I'll be right back!"

Sheriff Tom raced over to the zombies, and Emma did what anybody would do in her position: she ran like hell, and hoped to find the group fast.

Eric was walking behind Ringo, calling out for Billy and Jimmy. No one had noticed Emma was missing yet. She could hear Eric, and tried to follow the sound of his voice, wary of every shadow and sound. Without her gun she was helpless.

After Sheriff Tom had destroyed the zombies that threatened to interrupt his next murder, he got back to the tree and nearly exploded with rage when he saw that Emma was gone. He knew he should have stuck her to the tree with his blade for safe-keeping, and kicking himself for not doing so.

"No one fucks with Sheriff Tom!" He snarled, racing off into the woods to find Emma.

"Randy, can you meet us at Mary's house in twenty minutes?" Billy said, checking the time on his phone.

"Yeah, we'll be right there."

"Watch out for zombies." Billy's voice was low and serious. "They're everywhere." He was more than a little worried about everything turning out the way they needed it to.

Billy felt something tapping on his shoulder and jumped, shouting in fear and pulling out his gun.

"Did I scare you, bitch." Jimmy waved his gun at him sideways, trying to act like a 'gangsta'. "Look at my new tattoo." His sleeve was rolled up, so pointed the gun at his forearm, which now had a tribal tattoo on it.

"When'd you get a tattoo?" Billy asked, confused. Then he looked closer and saw that it was a fake nylon sleeve with the tattoo on it. He shook his head and grinned. "Jimmy, I called everybody and nobody wants to help us except for Randy and his fuckin' friend."

"Fuck it." Jimmy said slipping his gun into his pocket.

"Yeah, fuck it!" Billy overdramatized. "Fuck the zombies and everything we've been through together already." He shook his head, totally stressed out. "Let's find the group. We've got to get to Mary's house and meet Randy and his fuckin' friend."

*****

"Billy!" Kristen shouted, holding up her pistol and walking carefully behind Eric and Ringo.

"I don't see him or Jimmy anywhere." Randall was walking with her back to Kristen. "Hey guys wait," she looked around, "where did Emma go?"

"Fuck!" Eric shouted, looking around frantically. "Emma, Emma!" He ran, trying to find his sister, praying silently that he'd find her before something happened to her.

"These guys must be fuckin' idiots to separate from the group at this time." Ringo muttered.

"We need to find them now!" Eric said, walking through the group and ahead of them. He picked up his pace and without realizing it, slammed right into Sheriff Tom. He bounced off him and fell flat.

"You're fucked!" Sheriff Tom growled. He started to laugh maniacally while Eric tried to get to his feet.

"Get down Eric!" Ringo shouted, leveling his gun at the sheriff and firing off a couple of rounds.

The shots missed the sheriff, and he stood there laughing at them all, holding his own shotgun in one hand and a long knife in the other.

"It's all good!" Sheriff Tom shouted with a huge smile on his face.

He didn't see Billy and Jimmy coming up behind him. Jimmy was on Billy's shoulders, riding piggyback, holding a brick and Billy was running straight toward Sheriff Tom. The two of them were screaming wildly hoping to distract the sheriff. When Jimmy was in reach of him, he swung the brick as hard as he could, and hit Sheriff Tom squarely on the back of his head.

There was a loud 'Thump', and then Sheriff Tom fell.

TEN

"Holy shit!" Eric looked down at the unconscious Sheriff Tom in shock. "You got him!"

The whole group had formed a circle around the sheriff. All of them were looking down at him, making the group look like a very strange looking football team in a huddle.

"Well, we both got 'em." Billy sounded slightly cocky but he was making light of it just so no one knew how scared he actually was. "He was comin' after you guys, we had to do something. I wonder what's under that eye patch."

Billy crouched down and nervously slipped off the eye patch. He stood up looking at it, and then sniffed it, totally grossing everyone out.

"Smells like chocolate." He shoved it under Jimmy's nose and he nodded. Kristen smacked his arm and he shook his head smiling and dropping the eye patch back on the sheriff.

"I'd still fuck it." Jimmy joked.

"That's just gross." Randall made a face, staring at Jimmy.

"You're crazy as shit, man." Eric said, staring down at the sheriff.

"I can't believe its Sheriff Tom." Kristen shook her head and leaned closer to Billy.

"I told you I saw that nut bag earlier." Ringo said.

"Who's this fuckin' guy?" Billy pointed at Ringo.

"This is Ringo." He pointed a thumb at him. "He lives here in the woods. He gonna help us."

"But-" Billy raised his hand, wanting to say more but was cut off by Eric.

"No more questions," he said. "We need to figure out what we're going to do with Sheriff Tom."

"What the fuck is he?" Randall asked, looking from Sheriff Tom to Eric.

"He's a motherfucker." Jimmy stammered.

"Yeah Jimmy, he is that." Eric nodded. "But he's something else."

"He's some kind of monster." Billy said.

Sheriff Tom looked at peace lying there. Except for the area around and where his eye used to be, he looked quite normal. That entire area, a black crusted section of his face, looked horrid. It looked like a hardened scab that never went away, as if it had grown that way not because of the eye being torn out of his face, but because the damage was done by something evil, and part of that evil was now inside him.

Lying unconscious there as he was, the rage had subsided and his mind was able to relax and truly dream for the first time in at least the past year. His dreams brought him back many years to when he was a younger man trying to deal with the many things he had lost.

It was a time when his life was swirling with confusion, after his daughter Becky had died; drowned in the family pool. He was visiting the cemetery when Arleen and her young daughter Mary had shown up. Even though their affair had ended, for the first time, a couple of years prior, Arleen told him she was concerned. She said she wanted to make sure the he was alright, and spoke to him about how sorry she was regarding his recent divorce as well as the loss of his daughter.

It was a beautiful Spring day, and even though the sheriff was happy to see Arleen and her daughter, he felt a bit uncomfortable because their relationship had ended.

"Don't go too far honey." Arleen called out to Mary as the little girl walked down a line of tomb stones.

Mary was very curious about tomb stones. It was the first tie she'd ever seen any, and even though she could read some of the names on them, she liked to look at the designs carved into them and read the dates.

"She is somethin'," Arleen smiled happily at Tom, who was leaning on his daughter's grave stone.

"That's for sure." He nodded, grinning at how much Mary looked like her mother. It made him think of his own daughter, and how much he missed her; the smile, the laugh, the silly things she used to do.

"I just haven't been the same ever since I lost Becky. I still can't believe she's gone." He hung his head and tried to keep himself together.

"I know it's been hard, but I have to tell you something." Arleen looked at him seriously.

*****

Mary felt the cool breeze on her face and stood in the glare of the sun with her eyes closed, just soaking it like she would in the back yard at home.

"Mary." She heard a voice calling her. She could tell it was a girl's voice, and that she wasn't much older just by the sound of it, but she didn't see anyone around.

"Mary." She heard the voice call again. "Over here Mary." She followed the sound and saw a girl, slightly taller than her standing there in of the aisle, tombstones lined up on both sides like dominos ready to fall.

"Hi Mary." Mary thought the girl's voice was strange. She heard it with her ears, but also in her head too. "Wanna play hide and seek?" She asked.

"Sure," Mary said, running off to get away from her as much as to play the game.

"Run as fast as you can." She heard the girl say behind her after she took off through the rows of tombstones.

Mary ran as fast as she could, finding a very wide tree where she hid, for a second to catch her breath before moving on to a tall headstone that cast a shadow large enough to cover her. She pressed her body against it, feeling the cool surface of the stone through the back of her shirt. She could hear the other girl calling to her again. It was odd that she never said her name, and Mary didn't think to ask because somehow she felt as if she knew the girl, and didn't need to know her name.

After waiting a few minutes, she peeked around the side of the headstone she hid behind. The girl was there, but she was different somehow.

She was a zombie.

Mary remembered what zombies were from Halloween. But her mom told her there was no such thing as real zombies, it was all pretend.

'But Mommy hasn't seen this girl!' She thought to herself, shuddering in fear, 'She's real! She's really real!'

"Hi Mary!" the girl said, snarling at her.

Mary screamed a high pitched sound and ran.

*****

"You know you did this." Arleen sounded annoyed and hurt. Their conversation hadn't gone well since Mary had taken her. "You have to bare some responsibility for this."

"How do we even know that she's mine?" Tom said, standing up from the tombstone, holding his arms out. "She could really be anybodies."

Arleen couldn't hold back the rage and slapped Tom across the face before she could stop herself.

Tom shook his head, turned back around and leaned on the stone again. He didn't know what to think.

That was when they both heard her scream.

Mary came running over to them, slamming right into her mother, and holding onto her so tightly that Arleen nearly lost her balance.

"What's wrong honey?" Arleen looked down at her.

"Mommy, mommy, I saw a zombie!" She shouted, squeezing even tighter.

"A zombie-" She said, looking at Tom.

"I don't see it," he said, not sure if he was talking about the zombie in the cemetery or something that Arleen had brought to his attention. He walked off to try to find what had scared Mary so terribly while Arleen tried to comfort her.

*****

"I don't think that he's a zombie." Eric still held his gun close, in case he needed to use it on Sheriff Tom, who was still lying on the ground unconscious.

The sheriff had a grin on his face, almost a happy expression. Then all of a sudden he shook his head, and muttered, 'Mary'. The group jumped back a bit at the sudden sound, holding their guns in his direction.

"Whatever he is," Eric was still on edge, pointing his gun at the sheriff's head. "He's not human anymore. We should tie him up or something. He won't be out much longer."

"No." Kristen looked at him sternly. "We don't have time for that shit. We have to get to Mary's house."

"Randy told me that on the phone." Billy said in agreement, absently waving his gun in the air.

"Let's just go to the van." Randall said, already turning away.

Eric tried to keep thoughts of his sister out of his head. He hoped they would run into her along the way back to the van and she'd be fine, or at worst, return to normal after the spell was reversed. He clutched the book and his gun, running to keep up with Ringo, who had taken the lead again.

*****

Molly, still possessed by Mary Horror, headed to the house of the only other witch that she knew of in life, and eventually found herself knocking on the door to the 'Witch of Garibaldi Street's' door.

"Can I help you with something?" The witch, and older woman dressed in black asked, when she saw Molly standing there. She hadn't noticed the cleaver as Molly pushed her way through the door.

"Where's my book?" Molly's voice was an eerie sound that echoes in the room.

"What book?" The witch asked, confused. "Who are you?"

Molly swung the cleaver up.

"You bitch!" The witch shouted, seeing the blade coming down and helpless to do anything to stop it as the sharp edge of the blade slashed through her throat.

Blade gushed out of the jagged wound and the witch fell to the floor, unable to even cry for help as her life flowed out of her.

Molly left the small house and began walking down the street. There was a female zombie coming at her. Even though she was a zombie, Mary, in Molly's tired body, needed a change. She allowed the zombie to approach her and abruptly left Molly's body to enter hers.

Molly dropped the cleaver and fell to the street. The female zombie shook violently as Mary entered her body, then lifted up the cleaver and continued on down the street.

ELEVEN

Ringo led the group through the woods to the docks. The light strung around the area were still on, showing the van still parked exactly where they left.

"Eric, do you still have the spell book?" Kristen asked, running out of the woods.

"Yeah, I still have it." Eric confirmed breathlessly, running down to the van.

When the group reached the van, Kristen tried to slide open the side door, and jumped, screaming when Emma's face suddenly appeared in the window. Eric followed suit, but he was so shocked he tossed the spell book in the air. He heard a splash behind him as he held his gun with both hands and pointed it at the van window.

"Where the fuck have you guys been?" Emma shouted form inside the van.

It took a moment for everyone to breathe easy again. Ringo stepped over to the van and slid the door open. Emma got and he put an arm around her swept her close to him. She smiled at him, surprised at his sudden showing of affection.

"I'll be back baby, I've got to drain the main vain." His voice sounded extra- deep and gravely.

"What the fuck's a 'main vain'?" Billy made a face and asked Jimmy, who was standing next to him.

"Oh Billy, it's your cock," Jimmy said casually.

"Fuck, no." Eric stared out at the lake, looking pale.

"What wrong?" Randall came up behind him.

"It slipped," Eric sounded nervous and tongue-tied, struggling to get his words out. "Emma," he pointed back to the van, "the book, and it-"

"Eric where's the book?" Randall demanded.

"It's in the lake." Eric pointed to the water.

"The sheriff got me." Emma stood alone at the van, gesturing over to Billy, Jimmy and Kristen. "I just wanted to let you guys know."

"What?" Billy looked confused. "But we just knocked him out in the woods back there."

"Hey guys," Randall called out to them. "He lost the book. It's in the lake."

She saw Eric walking toward the water as the rest of the group came up behind her.

"No, no, no, no, no," she said running over to him.

"What did she just say?" Billy sounded out of breath.

"Book's in the lake," Emma pointed, sounding too tired to care anymore.

"What do we do now?" Kristen threw her hands up in the air.

"Fuck-" Billy mumbled.

Ringo had walked back into the woods, but instead of taking a piss like he'd said he was going to do, he took out his phone.

"Marty, Ringo reporting." He kept an eye out to make sure that no one had followed him while he spoke. "They're bringing the book to Mary's house." He shook his head, listening to Marty, than grinned. "Got it. Over and out." He slipped the phone back into his pocket and walked back to the group.

He wondered what was going on when he saw them all standing by the lake. 'They should be in the van ready to go.' He thought to himself. 'These guys would never have survived the military.' He thought.

"No, I'll go in." Randall grabbed Eric should to stop him.

"You can't." He said roughly, pulling away from her.

"Why not?"

"Because the lake smells like balls soup." It was the first thing that came to his mind so he said it, just so she wouldn't go.

"Balls soup." She faced him, realizing what he was trying to do and thought it was sweet.

"Yeah, the lake smells like balls." He stepped closer to Randall and she put her hand on the side of his face.

"Eric," she managed to say, right before she kissed him.

Suddenly she pushed him away, rushing into the water. She took a quick breath and dove in

"What the hell is she doing?" Billy asked.

"I saw it!" Randall said jumping up from the water. "Just one more time." She held up a finger, took another deep breath and dove back in. The red symbol on the cover of the book shined light a beacon, leading her right to it. It didn't take much for her to grab it and get back to the surface again.

She shook her head and wiped the water out of her eyes, thinking that Eric was right the lake did smell like balls soup. She craved a long hot shower when the day was done.

"I got it." She held the book up, then tossed it onto the sand right in front of the group.

"She got it!" Billy said.

All of a sudden there was a wave and splash in the water behind Randall and Sheriff Tom was standing there.

"Randall, behind you!" Eric shouted.

But it was too late. Sheriff Tom grabbed her and threw her in the water, growling and snarling as he held her struggling form down.

"I gotta get down there!" Eric ran toward them.

"Eric, no!" Kristen yelled. She and Emma tried to hold him back but couldn't.

Billy and Jimmy ran straight for the van. Ringo had just gotten there himself, hold his rifle as if he were about to fire it.

"What the fuck just happened?" He shouted at them.

"Randall's dead, and Sheriff Tom's in the lake." Billy said in a rush. "We gotta get out of here!"

Ringo open the driver's side door to the van.

"He was lookin' at us like he wanted to fuck us Jimmy!" Billy shouted fearfully.

"Ah, the fuckin' battery's dead." Ringo slammed the door shut. "Let's go soldiers; we gotta make it on foot."

"We gotta get the rest of them!" Billy yelled.

"C'mon!" Ringo roared, running toward the group.

Kristen and Emma finally got a good hold on Eric, and managed to pull him away from the water.

"I can't leave her! I can't!" He shouted, in tears. "Please come back!"

Randall's body floated in the lake, and Sheriff Tom was suddenly nowhere to be seen.

Then Billy and Jimmy were there, with Ringo close behind searching for any sign of the sheriff.

"Eric, we gotta go!" Billy said.

"Let's go, if we don't move we're gonna die." He looked at Eric. "So get your shit and go, c'mon!"

Eric got his gun and the book. He held the book tightly to his chest, never wanting to lose sight of it again because of what he just lost. He caught up with the rest of them in no time.

"Wait, wait!" He yelled to them when they reached the boathouse. "I can't leave Randall, not like that."

"Eric, we'll get her when all this is over, I promise." Kristen said when she caught her breath.

Billy walked over to him and put his hand on Eric's shoulder.

"Listen, I know she had a nice ass, but we've got to get that book to Mary's house." He pointed at it, sounding frustrated. "And end this shit!"

"Now that's what I'm talking about soldier, let's go." Ringo stood away from the rest, holding his rifle arm up so the gun would rest casually against his shoulder.

"Fine." Eric said, defeated. "Maybe getting the book back in the house will reverse the spell and maybe she'll come back to life, I don't know."

"Alright, let's go." Emma grabbed him by the arm. "C'mon."

*****

"Billy needs our help, snap out of it!" Randy shouted inside the car, slapping Mike across the face.

"What about that bitch Mary? What if she shows up?" Mike looked fearfully at him.

"It'll be okay. We're going to help them end this nightmare once and for all." He said, determined. "I know we can stop it!"

TWELVE

Mary, in her new body, was hacking her way at couple of zombies in an alley near the library in Bernardsville when she saw them. They were normal people, untouched by the spell that had overwhelmed the town. There were six of them, but there was something odd about one of them, and then she felt something even stronger coming from them, something that seemed to call to her.

One of them had her spell book!

She left the alley to pursue them, gripping her cleaver tightly.

"I see nothing but zombies." Eric looked around the street they were on shaking his head.

"We just have to go through the parking lot to get to Rooftop Road." Kristen said nervously.

"I'm gonna fuck some zom-babes." Jimmy snickered.

"Yeah Jimmy," Billy slapped him on the back.

"What the fuck are you talkin' about?" Eric turned to them.

"Just stay close." Ringo said, picking up the pace a bit.

The group waded through a crowd of zombies that clogged the road, and then they were able to pick things up even more. They didn't see him lurking behind them

It was Sheriff Tom.

*****

The Night Hunters had begun to roam the town, dressed in black they moved unseen in the darkness, taking down zombies by the dozen. They passed through a small neighborhood where most of the residents went down easy, and there were even a couple of survivors that didn't turn because they were in their basements. Then they reached a barn.

"We've been safe so far because we've been smart." The man leading the group said just outside the door of the building. "Keep your fingers off the triggers until you see a target, and then aim for the head. Don't go crazy in there. Alright Lindsey, check it out."

"Never send a man to do a woman's job." She said in a huff.

"Just check it out." He replied, annoyed at her attitude.

Lindsey slid the door open about a foot, sliding in her flashlight and the barrel of her rifle. When she was sure that she didn't see anything move, or hear any of the typical noises that came form the walking dead, she pulled away.

"Clear," she nodded at their leader.

"Alright, ready?" The leader asked. When he was sure everyone had responded in kind, his grabbed the handle of the door. "Let's clear this out."

The door slid open, echoing loudly. The group consisted of five men and two women. All of them were armed to the teeth and wearing body armor to protect them against bites. The entered the barn like a well-oiled machine.

"Check those corners." The leader gestured toward them using the barrel of his gun.

"You got it." One of them responded, slowly moving away from the rest to shine his light in the far corners.

A shape, shrouded in shadows, ran across the open area in front of them.

"Hold it!" One of the men in the front row held up his fist. "Who let the zombies out?" He joked, raising his rifle.

"I got this, another man said, moving up through the middle of the group.

"Cover him," the leader said to the rest of them.

The Hunter walked to the side of the barn without incident. When he got to the far corner, he light shined on a young girl, obviously a zombie, because she was eating a piece of raw flesh resembling a hunk of a person's arm or leg.

"Oh fuck." He said calmly, taking aim. He fired a second later, taking it down with a bullet to the head before the creature had a chance to come after him.

"Got that bitch." He said returning to the rest of them.

Another zombie ran past them, heading for a back door. Lindsey took it down with her revolver before she could make it.

"Did you see the tits on that one?" She smiled at the man crouched down next to her.

"Who didn't," he smirked.

"Come on, keep up." The leader said, walking them further in.

"What the fuck is happening here?" One of them asked.

"I didn't sign up for this shit." The man next to Lindsey said.

"I did," one of the guys behind him laughed.

"You ready?" The leader asked the group.

"Yeah, we got you covered." The other man in the lead declared.

He slid the back door of the barn open, and there were more zombies there. The group took them down, with the nearest coming very close to them before being shot down by nearly the entire group.

"Stop, hold your fire, I think she's dead." The man in the lead said. "Call in the vans. We've got to dispose of all of these bodies."

One of the men ran off to make the call.

"Let's move out." The leader said, taking them back outside.

*****

Ringo led the group to the parking lot, where they all crouched down behind a couple of cars.

"Zombies, at twelve-o'clock." Billy said after standing for a quick second to check out the area.

"I got 'em." Ringo stepped away from the group, leaving them behind the cars and moving into the open area.

He heard a noise by one of the cars, and bent down to check it out when a female zombie covered in tattoos and on roller-skates silently came up on him. He stood up but couldn't raise his gun in time.

The zombie sunk her teeth into Ringo's throat, biting deeply and shaking her head like a dog would while playing with a sock that had a knot tied in it. Blood started to gush as the zombie tore a piece of flesh away. Ringo's throat became a fountain of blood as he sunk to the ground, holding his neck and slowly dying. He tried to raise his gun, but there was no strength left in his arm to do it.

"Ringo!" Eric shouted, standing up.

The rest of the group follow suit, with Emma covering her mouth when she saw Ringo go down.

"Run!" Eric shouted.

Ringo felt his life ebbing away as the zombie rolled away from him. He felt terrible for failing the group, as well as his father, but there was nothing he could do about.

"Ringo, over and out," he uttered, nearly inaudibly as he took his last breath.

Another nearby zombie saw Ringo, and she started to walk toward his body.

"Fresh meat!" she said, clearly excited.

THIRTEEN

Randy flipped his hair back to make sure it looked perfect and stared at Mike.

"Are you rolling Mike?" He sighed, still thinking that Mike was slower than molasses.

"Yes I'm rolling," he said, squinting into the camera, standing a few feet in front of Randy.

"Welcome back ladies and gentlemen. Right now I'm out in front of Mary Horror's house." He pointed to the house behind him, and the zombies walking all around. "As you can see just behind me lies a seething pit of evil. A lot has been going on since my last broadcast. I am now convinced that Mary is alive. I've seen her spirit take possession of another woman's body, and she's been using it as a vessel to walk around and kill. Also on top of that, something else has been happening here in Bernardsville. Zombies are on the loose everywhere, and people are being slaughtered on the streets like cattle."

Mary Horror, in the zombie body that she's possessing, runs up behind Randy and hacks at him with her cleaver.

Randy had no idea she was there and shrieks in pain as Mary cuts into him, hacking at his back. His mouth fills with blood and he goes down, falling onto the lawn.

"Holy shit!" Mike shouted. He pulled his face away from the camera, and cursed under his breath when he saw that there was nothing he could do to save Randy.

The 'Mary-zombie' turns toward Mike. He tried to back-pedal out of there but slipped up and ended up on the ground too.

"Please don't kill me!" He pleaded. "I can make you famous."

The cleaver hit him repeatedly, with Mary grunting each time blood was drawn.

The camera was still rolling.

The five remaining members of the group finally reached Mary's house, running up on the lawn just in time to see Randy and Mike take their last breaths.

"Randy!" Billy yelled when he saw their bodies.

"Who killed them?" Eric wondered out loud.

"Who the fuck cares," Kristen started shooting at the zombies coming up behind them, "they're getting closer."

"Let's get going," Emma pushed Billy forward.

They all ran, never noticing Sheriff Tom coming up behind them. He took his time, knowing they were going to stop eventually, and when they did he'd get them, and he'd get the spell book back as well.

"Now what?" Eric asked when they got to the front door of the house.

"Give me the book, I'm going in!" Billy said bravely. He was determined to end the spell any way possible.

"Good luck," Eric handed him the spell book. "We'll cover you."

"Jimmy, you're coming with me." Billy looked unyieldingly at his best friend, who walked over to his side. Billy put his arm over his shoulder and nodded. "We got this!"

Suddenly there was a small explosion on the porch in front of the door. A dark cloud formed and as it quickly dissipated a short figure emerged, standing there wearing a dark hooded cloak.

"Who the fuck is that Jimmy?" Billy said wild-eyed.

The figure raised its arms, exposing long boney fingers with long sharp nails. The hands shook, and visible tendrils of energy shot out of them and at Billy. The energy hit the spell book, and like a fish with a hook in it, the spell book was pulled from his grasp and into the hands of the dark figure.

"Holy shit!" Billy clutched down on Jimmy's shoulder. "Let's get the fuck out of here!"

"We've got to get out of here." Emma shouts, following close behind Billy and Jimmy.

The shrouded figure flips through pages of the spell book as a crowd of zombies head up to the front lawn of Mary's house led by Sheriff Tom.

Eric is furious that the sheriff has followed them. He wants him dead for murdering Randall, and without saying a word or thinking of the consequences, runs toward him.

Kristen was standing next to Eric when he ran off. She felt an odd tapping sensation on her shoulder. She turned to see what it was and gasped in horror.

It was the Mary in her zombie body.

The last thing Kristen saw was the clear coming down at her.

*****

"What was that guy?" Billy asked, stopping at the side of the house to sit on a step and catch his breath. "A weirdo! Oh, goddamn zombies again," he swung his arms in frustration when he saw a group of the undead approaching.

"Fuck no, I'm over this shit!" Emma cocked her pistol and went after them.

"I got shot Billy." Jimmy said his arms crossed protectively over his chest.

"What?" Billy was in panic mode. "You can't leave me! You can't leave me Jimmy."

*****

Sheriff Tom saw Eric coming toward him as he approached the house. He felt the rage building up inside him and knew right where he was going to release some of it.

"Come out here boy," he shouted to Eric. "Give me back my book!"

"Come get it you mutant-Mr. Clean-psycho-motherfucker!" Eric charged at Sheriff Tom, punching him in the stomach, but it felt like he hit a brick wall. He was about to fire at him when the sheriff grabbed him by the throat and lifted him off the ground. He tossed him aside like a child would throw a toy.

Eric landed on his back and scrambled to a sitting position, aiming his gun directly at Sheriff Tom.

"This is for Randall!" He said, shooting the sheriff right in the chest.

The sheriff laughed it off and stepped toward him, but before he could get any closer the surrounding zombies came at him. He was attacked from all sides and taken down to the ground growling and shouting.

Eric saw Kristen lying on the ground a few feet away. He crawled over to her.

"Kristen! Kristen! What happened," he said frantically. "Did you pass out? Kristen wake up!"

Kristen's eye shot open, but there was no expression on her face, just a blank stare. She sat up mechanically and grabbed the clear that was in the grass next to her. She looked at Eric, who was still calling her name and trying to get her attention, and grabbed him by the shirt. With a quick powerful movement, she pulled him down toward her, and the cleaver she held in her other hand.

The blade sunk deeply into Eric's abdomen. Blood came out of his mouth as she flung him aside and stood up, still carrying the cleaver.

Silently, Kristen walked away.

*****

"Let me see that wound." Billy said, moving Jimmy's hands out of the way. "What the hell is that thing?" he said, poking around in Jimmy's coat. "What is this?" he asked, pulling out some sort of wrapper. When he looked it over he saw that it was a ketchup packet that must have burst. "It's fuckin' ketchup! It's ketchup!" Billy shouted at him.

"Yeah, but I'm still a goner." Kimmy insisted.

In front of them Emma battles zombies, kicking punching and shooting them.

"You put this in your damn jacket when we were eating that food before!" Billy shouted.

*****

Kristen, possessed by Mary, walked to the front of the house. She was about to walk up the stairs when she saw the cloaked man standing there holding her spell book. Confused, she just stood there.

The shadowy figure raised his free hand and his fingers pulsed with energy. He gestured at Kristen as if he were clutching at something unseen, then tendrils of energy formed again, stretching out between him and Kristen, sinking into her and pulling Mary out of her body.

The energy crackled with life as Kristen fell on the ground, empty of Mary, but still unconscious after being knocked out by the flat side of Mary's cleaver.

The cloaked man's hand glowed with power, and he thrust the hand into the spell book, sending the power into it. He then flipped the book closed and stepped forward on the porch, facing the front lawn where Sheriff Tom was being ripped apart by a horde of zombies.

He began to recite a spell with a voice that's sounds like fire and lightning.

May the dead become the living and become whole again.
May the dead become the living and become whole again.
May the dead become the living and become whole again.

As the last word of the spell was said, the horde of zombies around Sheriff Tom fell to the ground, healed and normal again. Other than his eye, Sheriff Tom himself was even healed, lying unconscious on the ground.

*****

Sheriff Tom found himself in front of a long table. It was covered in a white tablecloth and set for a meal, but there was no food on it. Only the spell book.

He looked down at himself, and saw that he was dressed in normal clothing, a white shirt and khakis. 'A lot more comfortable than my uniform.' He thought to himself. Then he realized he could see out of both eyes. "Holy shit, my eye!" he said, touching his face just to make certain it was, in fact there. "This can't be real!"

"Bring the book back to Salem, Daddy." It was Becky's voice.

"Becky!" He said, looking around for her.

"Get the book, Daddy, it's yours." Becky said. She materialized sitting across the table from him, smiling. "Bring the book to Salem Daddy."

Tom felt tears form in his eyes. Seeing his daughter, alive again and wearing a white dress just broke his heart.

"Dinner time." Arleen said, coming up behind him with a plate. The spell book was on it.

"Arleen." He whispered urgently.

"Listen to your daughter," she said, rubbing his should and looking at him with a passion he remembered well. "Bring the book back to Salem. Bring the book back to Salem. Bring the book, back to Salem. Put an end to all this." She kissed the side of his head and walked away.

'Arleen said that as if it were some sort of spell.' Sheriff Tom thought, feeling like he was going insane.

"Sheriff, y'know, you're not lookin' all that well." Dr. Hess said, standing at the head of the table. "I would write you a prescription but, I'm dead."

"I'm afraid you're losing you head sheriff." Kim said, sitting next to him. She looked as young and beautiful as ever, which Sheriff Tom knew could be true, because she was also dead.

"What the fuck?" he said, pushing his chair away from the table.

Suddenly Mayor Grafton was sitting at the table with him, smoking a cigar.

"Tom, stop being a fucking asshole." He said, exhaling a thick cloud of smoke.

He saw Mary sitting across from him. She was so young, just like that day in the cemetery.

"You know you are my Daddy," she said pointing at him as she said each word.

He felt himself panic. 'How does Mary know? She couldn't have heard her mother and I talking that day?'

Suddenly they were all there at the same time, saying the same thing over and over again, like a cursed mantra.

"No more!" he shouted, covering his ears with his hands.

"Bring the book back to Salem!"

*****

The cloaked man stepped off the porch and walked over to Sheriff Tom amidst the unconscious bodies. He flipped back his hood to reveal that he was Marty.

"I have created a monster." He said in a gravelly voice. "I have no use for you anymore." He angrily pointed down at Sheriff Tom. "Your job is finished, it is done!" He turned and walked away.

Sheriff Tom woke, and sat up straight. He saw Marty walking away and stood up, aiming his shotgun at him.

"I'm not done yet motherfucker!" He snarled.

"Oh shit!" Marty said, turning around to see the shotgun pointed at him.

Sheriff Tom fired, and Marty went down in a heap of blood and guts.

"At first I lost my little girl." He said. There was both anger and sadness in his voice. "Then the love of my life. Now you turned me into a monster!" He picked up Marty by the front of the cloak he was wearing. "This all ends now!" He snatched the spell book from Marty's hand and walked away.

Behind him, Marty's body faded into mist, leaving the empty cloak.

FOURTEEN

Billy, Jimmy and Emma were sitting on the stairs at the side of the house taking a breather after all their fighting. They were drinking a few beers they'd found in a cooler lying in the woods while fighting off the last of the zombies that were near them. They didn't yet know that the spell had been reversed.

"I think we should go back and help them, huh?" Billy asked Jimmy. "They're probably out there fighting. What do you think?" He looked at Emma, who was exhausted from everything that had happened. "You up for it?"

Emma smacked the beer bottle out of his hand and got up. Billy followed suit, with Jimmy a step behind.

"Let's do it." Billy stammered after belching loudly.

They got to the front of the house and were shocked to see all the zombies on the ground, but also Eric and Kristen.

Emma, seeing Eric bloody and on the ground raced to him as fast as she could, crying and calling his name.

Billy ran to Kristen's side with Jimmy there along with him.

"Billy I lost my bottle of beer!" Jimmy said when they reached her.

"Oh fuck the bottle, look Kristen's passed out!" He lightly tapped her face. "Wake up, wake up!"

He and Jimmy tried to sit her up. When they saw that she was moving one her own, they let go of her.

"She's alright Jimmy!" Billy followed them over to where Eric and Emma were. "Oh shit!" he said when he saw the state that Eric was in.

"He's dead!" Emma shouted hysterically.

"Come on Emma!" Billy grabbed her arms and pulled her along. "We've got to keep moving, you can't die, and we've got to keep going."

*****

The news came on early that morning, and everyone was surprised to see what had happened in Bernardsville.

"It's New 25 with Lonnie Anderson and Marilyn Stone, with Chuck Marble out in the field. We're not zombies, we're back to normal. We now go to breaking news with Chuck Marble."

"Now that the zombie spell has been lifted, life is slowly getting back to normal here in the town of Bernardsville. There is one sad bit of news to report however, Mayor Rockland was found dead in his hotel room, the victim of an apparent zombie attack. I'm Chuck Marble, back to you Lonnie and Marilyn."

"Well it seems we're back to normal. And Marilyn, if I may say, you were delicious." Lonnie joked, with the camera cutting to show only Marilyn's head.

"Hm, I bet." She said smiling.

*****

The morning sun shined brightly on Billy, Kristen, and Jimmy and Emma. The four had become two couples during the last hours of the night, with them paired off and walking down the street together on their way home.

"What a crazy night fighting zombies Jimmy." Billy looked over at him, totally exhausted.

"Yeah well, we kicked some ass." Jimmy said.

"Yeah, we need a vacation. Billy snickered.

"William, we fuckin' do." He looked at Emma and smiled.

"Can we come?" She asked him, a little brighter than she'd been since her brother died.

"Sure, you guys can come." Billy answered, winking at her.

"I guess I won't be texting Tureeka anymore." Jimmy laughed.

"Tureeka?" Emma looked at him and made a face.

"Yeah." Jimmy nodded.

"I can't believe Mary entered my body." Kristen looked upset.

"I wonder what happened to Mary's body?" He grinned with his eyebrows raised, and she playfully smacked him and walked away.

"What?" Billy asked, following her.

Epilogue

Sheriff Tom was walking down a deserted street laughing. He's carrying Mary's cleaver, and the spell book as well as the shotgun he stole from Mayor Grafton's house.

"I'm home," He said, when he saw the sign for Salem, Massachusetts. "It's all good!"

Nick Kisella grew up in Manville, New Jersey, where he began writing fantasy and horror while attending high school. Some of his first published work appeared in the Indie magazines 'Dreadknight', and 'The Nocturnal Lyric'. Since then his work has appeared in various forms from print and online magazines to blogs. His first fantasy novel, 'The Emerald and the Blade' came out in 1989 by a long defunct publisher, with 'The Chalice of Souls' soon to follow. Some of his more recent work includes a screenplay and novelization for 'Nifty Entertainment' a California based Indie production company, as well as getting the first two fantasy novels he wrote as a teen, 'The Chalice of Souls' and 'Death and the Doomweaver' back in print for the sheer nostalgia of it. 'Morningstars', his first full-length horror novel was published by Black Bed Sheet Books in 2012. 'The Beasts and the Walking Dead' a post-apocalyptic fiction novel, has also been published by Black Bed Sheet Books and is the first part of a series. He wrote the novelization to the James Balsamo film, 'I Spill Your Guts', and recently finished penning the novelization for the Ryan Scott Weber films, 'Mary Horror' and 'Sheriff Tom Vs. the Zombies'. Always having an eventful life, he writes when time allows, usually after dark.

A fitness enthusiast, he has been a certified fitness instructor involved in the industry for twenty years, and continues to stay in shape and train individuals while well into his 40s.

Nick resides in rural Northwestern New Jersey with his wife and twins.

 Ryan Scott Weber (Born February 24, 1980) is an American film director, screenwriter, producer, cinematographer, actor, editor and musician. He shoots and produces many of his films in his native town of Bernardsville, New Jersey. Ryan began his interest in filmmaking at just 15 years old with an old VHS camcorder. Now, at the age of 33, he is the owner of Weber Pictures Company in New Jersey. Weber also plays the drums and has released two albums with the Trustkill Records band Crash Romeo in 2006 and 2008. For almost 15 years now he is still directing, editing, writing, producing, acting, drumming and shooting. Weber has a distinctive directorial style. He manages to make what looks like big budget movies for little money. Weber's first feature film, Mary Horror, was released in 2012 and he has recently completed the sequel Sheriff Tom Vs. The Zombies. Weber is a strong supporter of independent film and the conventions that are involved in this surrounding. Weber and his crew have attended and ventured over ten conventions in the last year and in October 2012; The Chiller Theatre Convention in Parsippany, NJ featured the film Mary Horror and also Sheriff Tom vs. The Zombies with two exclusive showings. Weber will continue to make independent films and ensures us the best is yet to come!